The Haze of Perception

By D.S. Brown

Printed in the United States of America

ISBN-10: 0578129167

ISBN-13: 978-0-578-12916-7

First Printing, 2013

Cover by: Kathleen M. Brown

This book is dedicated to M.

Your ever present smile never betrayed that you had been savagely raped as a child. Neither did the twinkle in your eyes convey the fear and confusion you felt as you were shuffled from home to home during the years you spent in foster care.

You were a shy teenager when you met H at church and soon married him. The two of you raised four children together. During those busy years you finished high school and went on to college. When you graduated from nursing school, we were so proud of you. We were not surprised when you decided to help others and relive what you had endured as a child by becoming a counselor.

When the only man that you ever loved lost his valiant battle with cancer, we mourned for H with you. Then suddenly our hearts were broken again when we were told that you had died instantly in an automobile accident.

Your bubbly personality lives on in your children and grandchildren. We are truly privileged and blessed to hold your memory in our hearts.

THE HAZE OF PERCEPTION
By: D. S. Brown
Chapter 1-Late September 1968

The random moments of intense fear and apprehension that had plagued Chelsea Jo Swanson during the recent months of her life were becoming less extreme with every mile she put between herself and Meadowview, New York. She was hoping that with the presence of God and the company of her late mother's little Boston Terrier, Sweetie, the rest of her trip would be enjoyable. And she was really looking forward to seeing her dad again when she got to his home in Florida.

She glanced at her watch and noticed that it was almost noon. Chelsea shivered when she realized that her former husband and his family would be waiting at the Civil War-era church in Meadowview, expecting her to walk down the isle to remarry him. She was shaking as she pulled her red 1960 Ford station wagon off of the road and into a gas station.

Chelsea stopped the car just as the attendant approached. She looked into the rear view mirror and caught a glimpse of the backseat. It was loaded with boxes full of her clothes and personal keepsakes. Behind that her mother's treadle Singer sewing machine took up a good portion of space in the very back of the station wagon. When her former husband, Michael, had asked her why the old sewing machine was in there, she hadn't even been able to look him in the eye when she told him that it needed to have some work done on it. She had withheld the fact that she was not going to remarry him because she was leaving Meadowview and taking the sewing machine with her to Florida. Knowing that the belt needed to be replaced didn't lessen her feeling of guilt for not having told him the whole truth.

She shook her head in the hope of dislodging any negative feelings just as the station's attendant began to fill her car's gas tank. With the dog's coaxing, she decided to stretch her legs. Sweetie's leash was safely attached, so the two of them walked to a grassy path. Once again, unwanted memories of Michael and his family invaded her thoughts. Chelsea had truly loved that man. But he had hurt her to the depth of her soul with his total neglect and constant infidelity. She had often wondered why his mother and sister never offered her any sympathy. But when she got to know them better, they reminded her of angry hornets. It seemed as though those two were capable of devouring a person with the stinging and biting words that spewed from their mouths.

Right in this very moment, Chelsea was certain that some very nasty things were being said about her. But for the comical antics of the dog, that thought would have overwhelmed her.

Chelsea didn't realize that she was smiling at Sweetie as they came walking back to her car. The attendant looked up and returned her smile then said, "Boston Terriers are a real entertaining breed of dog." She told the man that she had to agree then paid him. After she and Sweetie were back in her station wagon, she thanked God for bringing the slobbery-tongued animal into her life.

Only just yesterday she had taken the dog to visit the cemetery in Meadowview where Chelsea's mother was buried. Her mother hadn't chosen to share with her daughter that she had been experiencing heart problems, and that caused Chelsea to ache with sadness. But that was just like Darlene Langston Swanson. Chelsea knew that her mother loved her deeply. Yet her mother had always withheld a part of herself from everyone, including Chelsea.

When Chelsea had returned from the cemetery, she found Michael sitting in his truck outside her apartment and he was fuming with anger because he'd been waiting on her for a whole ten minutes. She had tried to explain to him that she had gone to the cemetery to visit her mother's grave because she wanted to tell her mother what was about to happen in her life. But his body language had made it perfectly clear to Chelsea that he wasn't at all interested in what she had to say. He had merely sniffed and snatched the apartment keys out of her hand.

After they were inside the apartment, Chelsea was determined to get her keys back. Very soon after he tossed them onto the kitchen table, she picked them up, went into the bedroom and hid them under the mattress. She didn't want anyone, including Michael, to enter that apartment until she was ready for it. And it was probably happening just about now!

Michael and his sister's husband, Asa Wilson, were probably breaking out the window in the only door to the apartment above Asa's garage. Chelsea was imagining Michael furiously charging in and finding everything neat and in its proper place. But he would be really surprised to find a huge sign hanging on the bedroom wall reading: TOUCHED YOU LAST!

Chelsea had often heard Michael's mother and sister say those words when they thought that they had gotten the best of someone in a business deal, especially if what they had done wasn't exactly on the up and up. With the exception of Michael's father, Henry Newton, the Newton Heating and Cooling Company was comprised of unethical scoundrels as far as Chelsea was concerned. Henry had tried repeatedly to make a responsible man out of his son, but Michael's mother, Cora, had always prevented that from happening.

Because Chelsea valued honesty, she was mentally struggling with her own conscience. Deep down she knew that she was guilty of letting Michael and his family believe that she would remarry him. She also realized that she was holding onto some very vengeful and unforgiving feelings towards them. The right thing to do would be to glorify God by asking for His forgiveness on behalf of the Newton family and herself. But hurt and anger were smothering her. Chelsea just couldn't feel any graciousness toward Michael and his family.

She was trying not to feel upset by these disconcerting thoughts while continuing to drive through Pennsylvania, but her mind wouldn't stop pulling out its memories. Soon Chelsea was thinking about her childhood. That time of her life had been for the most part very pleasant. Then out of the blue when she was fourteen, her parents sat her down and said they had something important to tell her. They both made it very clear how much they loved her. But then her mother told her that their marriage was over. Chelsea had been shocked and wondered why her father just sat there without saying a word. Later that same day he moved out of their home and into the apartment above his hardware store. Before he left, he told her that she could come over to see him whenever she wanted. Although Chelsea was heartbroken, she purposely hid her grief from her parents. All she wanted was for them to be happy, and if going their separate ways was what they both wanted Chelsea knew that she needed to accept their parting.

Chelsea had made time for each of her parents everyday. She had avoided becoming involved with extracurricular school activities so that she could help prepare and eat supper with her father on Mondays, Wednesdays and Fridays. She had done the same with her mother on Tuesdays, Thursdays and Saturdays. Because both of her parents had jobs, she tried to help them with the household chores. There were times when she felt torn between the two of them and her own needs and desires. She thought everything always seemed to work out and if she ever hurt either one of them, they had never said so.

Her father sold his business and the building that contained it not long before she graduated from high school in June of 1966. On the afternoon of her graduation, she and her parents went out to dinner together for the first time in years. Later Chelsea was thrilled when her dad accepted an invitation to have dessert and coffee with them in the small, two-bedroom cottage that her mother had purchased after the divorce. While casually sipping coffee her mother said, "Life is a series of changes." Chelsea had been caught off guard by what her mother said next. "Your father is moving to Florida. You need to decide whether to stay here in Meadowview with me or go with him." Both of her parents watched Chelsea's face go pale. That reaction had caused her father to softly say, "Perhaps you need some time to think about it, Chelsea. I'll be having a moving sale next week. Maybe you can help me with it while your mother's at work."

Chelsea had seen Sam Swanson look to Darlene for a clue as to what to do next, but he couldn't get his ex-wife's attention. While he watched Darlene gather the dessert dishes and cups, Chelsea knew for certain that her mother was deliberately avoiding his gaze. He looked totally dejected when he stood up and walked toward the front door. Chelsea gathered herself together enough to be able to follow and give him a good-bye hug. Then she promised to go over to his apartment later that afternoon.

After he left, Chelsea went into her bedroom to change from her pretty white graduation dress to her favorite T-shirt and shorts. She heard a soft knock on her bedroom door before her mother came in and said that she wanted to talk to her. Chelsea went over to her bed and sat cross-legged in the middle of it. She watched her mother walk over and pick up the hairbrush that was sitting on top of the dresser. Then her mother came and stood over her. Darlene began to brush her daughter's wavy, long brown hair. Chelsea could see the placid appearance on her mother's face being reflected in the mirror above the dresser so she wasn't prepared when her mother said in a hushed voice, "Sam Swanson isn't your real father."

Chelsea remembered feeling stunned while her mother calmly continued to brush her hair just as if she'd said nothing out of the ordinary. She had finally turned to look up at her mother and with words barely audible asked, "Mom, what are you talking about?"

Seemingly composed her mother had said, "In 1948 I was alone and pregnant at seventeen. My mother insisted that I should give my baby up for adoption." Darlene looked deep into her daughter's beautiful, brown eyes and emphatically said, "I didn't want to do that!" Then Darlene explained that her father had driven her to a bus station in Buffalo so that she could go to a home for unwed mothers. Two stops before that home, Darlene had gotten off the bus in Meadowview. Chelsea's mother said, "Your Grandmother Swanson found me crying at the bus stop and felt sorry for me. Lydia Swanson took me home with her and gave me a job working in her boarding house. She and Sam were very good to me. I'll always be grateful to them for their many kindnesses." She took a deep breath before saying, "During my fifth month of pregnancy, Sam asked me to marry him. I tried for years to love him, but I just couldn't!" Darlene looked tired and very sad as she slowly repeated, "I just couldn't."

Darlene looked thoughtful before she continued. "I always felt that I owed you the truth. But Sam convinced me that I should wait and tell you about your birth father when you were old enough to understand." Chelsea could see the love in her mother's eyes as she said, "While you were growing up, Sam's love for you was also growing. Eventually he asked me to never tell you about your real father." Darlene sighed and shook her head. Then she hugged Chelsea and said, "I'm sure these revelations must come as a shock to you and you must be feeling very confused. I'll leave you alone for now so that you can have some time to sort things out for yourself."

Left alone in her bedroom she had looked down at her hands and saw that they were trembling. Chelsea recalled picking up her lavender teddy bear with its peculiar bright yellow, glass button eyes and hugging it tightly. Her dad had given her the stuffed animal after he found out that she and her mother had painted Chelsea's bedroom in the cottage her favorite color, which was lavender. "My daddy," she had softly whispered. Then she realized that her mother hadn't told her anything about the man who had supposedly fathered her. It was in that moment that Chelsea wondered if she would ever want to know anything about her birth father because that could possibly be a betrayal to the only man that she would ever really think of as being her daddy.

Later that same afternoon she had taken the teddy bear with her to visit her daddy. When she got close enough, she could see that he was watching her approach. Chelsea didn't try to hide the fact that she was crying while tightly clutching the teddy bear that was a present to her from him. She stepped into his apartment and his only words were, "She told you." "Daddy, I love you," was all she could say through her tears. "I'm your father in every way that counts," was his gentle reply as he hugged the young woman who he truly considered to be his very own daughter.

Back then Chelsea had wondered if her father thought he could possibly lighten the mood by making them their favorite treat. He filled two sugar cones with vanilla ice cream and gave one to Chelsea. As he had handed her the cone she heard a tear in his voice when he said, "You'll always be my precious girl, Chelsea. Nothing will ever change that." She had also seen the tears welling up in his dark blue eyes that day and was still warmed with the understanding of the unbreakable bond that would forever hold them together.

As she continued driving toward Florida to start her new life, Chelsea kept remembering the afternoon of her graduation day. She recalled sitting at the kitchen table in her father's apartment and taking her first bite of that vanilla sugar cone. Tasting the ice cream triggered a memory of something that happened when she was eleven years old. Chelsea and her parents had picnicked at Lake Cleburne. That day she finished eating then walked down a small hill to sit by the edge of the lake. Soon her parents came and sat next to her. After a few minutes she heard her mother sharply say, "Stop it Sam!" Her father had looked so wounded. He merely put his arm around his wife's waist. Chelsea had asked what was wrong but neither had answered her. She had watched her mother get up then angrily storm back to the picnic table. Then her father left and went straight to the parking lot to wait in the car. Chelsea had been troubled by the incident, but as only a child can, she was soon preoccupied with the scrumptious taste of the vanilla ice cream in the sugar cone her daddy bought for her at an ice cream stand.

That night Chelsea had been awakened by the sounds of her parents' arguing. She thought she heard her father say, "Chelsea needs a baby brother or sister!" A door had slammed. Then Chelsea heard her mother crying in the bedroom next to hers. As the years had gone by, Chelsea slowly began to understand that she shouldn't have dismissed those incidents that she witnessed and overheard when she was eleven, because they indicated that all was not well with her parents' relationship.

The tires on her car seemed to be humming as they spun atop the surface of the pavement. Chelsea payed careful attention to her driving while pushing the unhappy memories out of her mind. But she couldn't keep herself from propelling those recollections of the afternoon on the day of her high school graduation into her thoughts. She had been sitting at the kitchen table in her father's apartment and eating that vanilla sugar cone when her lavender teddy bear fell onto the kitchen floor. Chelsea watched her father pick it up before he sadly said, "I just couldn't make your mother happy, and she never loved me. I would have done anything for her from the minute I saw her. I guess it was her platinum blond hair and those great, big blue eyes. Your mother was and still is so beautiful."

Sam sat starring out the window next to the table for a few moments before saying, "I fell in love with her the very first day that my mother brought her into our home. I knew that she didn't love me, but I asked her to marry me during her fifth month of pregnancy anyway. I suppose that was a foolish thing to do." After he had spoken those words, he looked so forlorn. Remembering the expression on his face was just as heartbreaking for Chelsea in this moment as it had been back then.

Chelsea drove passed the sign that said she was leaving the state of Pennsylvania and entering Maryland. She knew it was useless to try to expel her memories when they once again pulled her back to the afternoon of her high school graduation. She recalled that her dad had finished eating his sugar cone and seemed determined to keep talking. He said, "Your mother was overjoyed when you were born, but she kept telling me that she missed her father. I really thought it would be a good idea to take the two of you to Buffalo for a surprise visit with her family." Sam held his head in his hands as he looked down and said, "I couldn't have been more wrong." Dropping his hands, he looked up and said, "When Theo Langston opened his front door and saw his daughter, he immediately welcomed us into his home. If only your grandmother Langston would have been half as welcoming..." Sam's words had been left hanging but Chelsea got the full meaning of them.

"Your grandmother, Gloria, told your mother that she had disgraced the family, but Theo cut her off mid-sentence and said that what had happened was all in the past. Gloria never made an unkind remark to your mother during any of the other visits that we had with them after that. Then when you were two years old, your Granddad Theo passed away from a sudden heart attack. We wouldn't have even known about it if a friend of his hadn't phoned us. Your grandmother confronted Darlene right after Theo's funeral service and asked her to leave and never come back. Your mother was crushed. I tried to smooth things over, but your mother was never the same after that." Sam shook his head and said, "What a piece of work Gloria Langston was. I really believe that she is at least partly responsible for your mother's inability to ever be happy. She was such a critical old witch."

Chelsea was surprised by his words, because she had never heard her dad speak so unkindly of anyone ever before. Then she felt her stomach do a flipflop when he asked, "Did your mother tell you about your birth father?" Chelsea shook her head no. "Are you going to ask her?" She shrugged her shoulders. "Do you want to know about him?" He studied her intently then said, "I can see that you're unsure, but after all these years I finally understand that your mother was right. You do deserve to know the truth. I should have let her tell you years ago."

Her father had seemed very determined to keep talking when he took a deep breath and said, "Soon after your mother confided to her father that she was pregnant, he wanted to track down your birth father. The guy had told your mother that his name was Tony Peterson. He said that he worked at a dry-cleaning establishment down the street from the jewelry store where your mother was working part-time. Your Grandfather, Theo, decided to go and have a talk with Tony Peterson, but he met the owner of the dry-cleaning establishment instead. That's where the name Peterson comes into play. Peterson was the last name of the man who actually owned the dry-cleaning business. Mr. Peterson told Theo that your birth father's real name was Tony De Salvo. Mr. Peterson also said that De Salvo was engaged to be married to his own daughter, Ellen. But right after De Salvo gave Ellen Peterson an engagement ring, he ran off. Theo thought he should tell Mr. Peterson that De Salvo had impregnated your mother, so he did. The two of them surmised that De Salvo had gone into the jewelry store where your mother worked to buy an engagement ring for Mr. Peterson's daughter and that's when De Salvo and your mother met and became involved. A short time later your mother realized that she was pregnant, and she told De Salvo. That's when he disappeared.

Theo told me that he and Mr. Peterson went to De Salvo's apartment and asked his landlady if she knew where he was. She said that she thought he had gone back to Cleveland, Ohio, because he had relatives there. Peterson said that he was going to go to Cleveland and asked Theo if he wanted to go with him. But your granddad decided that the guy just wasn't worth the trouble." Chelsea asked, "Why did Mr. Peterson want to go after him?" Sam softly said, "Because the Peterson girl was pregnant, too."

Sam said, "Your Grandmother Langston insisted that Darlene should go to a home for unwed mothers and give her baby up for adoption. Against his better judgment, Theo went along with it." Sam smiled and said, "I'm glad your mother decided not to do that." Then he softly said, "I wish Theo hadn't died. He was the one person who could have kept things from falling apart."

While walking back to her mother's cottage on the evening of her high school graduation, Chelsea had realized two things. The first concerned her Grandfather Langston. Because of what her dad had said about him, she understood that just one person really could make a difference. She also realized that she didn't want to hear anymore about the circumstances of her conception. She was feeling very, very tired. All she really wanted to do was go to bed. But the minute she walked in the front door her mother said, "Come and sit down next to me, Chelsea. I'll tell you about your real father."

Chelsea recalled that she felt angry when she heard the words, real father. Immediately she told her mother that her dad had already given her all the information that she needed to know about her birth father. Then she had instantly regretted the harsh tone of her voice. She had tried to sound less severe when she sat down on the couch next to her mother and softly said, "Mother, I'd be happy to listen to what you want to tell me."

Darlene had caressed her daughter's hair and said, "You look like him. You have his big brown eyes and wavy, dark brown hair." Then her mother had sounded so sad as she looked down at her hands and said, "I loved him and thought that he loved me. He broke my heart when he just seemed to disappear after I told him that I was pregnant."

Her mother told Chelsea what few things Darlene actually knew about Anthony De Salvo, which wasn't much more than his name. She said that Tony De Salvo's favorite color was purple and that he liked drinking soda pop. Chelsea remembered being intrigued when she heard that her birth father's favorite color was purple since her favorite color was lavender. She thought about it for a few seconds then Chelsea decided not to tell her mother that she knew Tony De Salvo had lied when he said that his last name was Peterson.

Darlene gently cupped Chelsea's face in her hands and looked into her eyes before saying, "You're all that I have, Chelsea. Please don't go to Florida. There's an opening at the bank where I work. If you stay here, I'll do what I can to help you get a job there."

That night Chelsea's tumultuous emotions and confusion had prevented her from resting peacefully. She awakened the next morning feeling groggy. The very first thing she thought about was her high school graduation on the previous day. Chelsea felt good because she had accomplished something very momentous. But that feeling was short-lived when she remembered everything that happened following her graduation ceremony. Negative feelings began to envelope her so she decided to go and see her daddy. He'd always had a way of making her feel good no matter what was happening.

Chelsea arrived at his apartment over the hardware store and found him preparing for the moving sale. She looked into a cardboard box and noticed that he had kept many of her school papers and a plaster mold with the imprint of her little five-year old hand. When she asked her father how she could help, he told her that she could scrub the inside of the kitchen cupboard. After cleaning it, she looked around the apartment and noticed what few possessions her father actually had. Chelsea finally realized that after their divorce, her dad had given nearly everything to her mother. She thought she should have been aware of this before and felt a little guilty because she hadn't.

Later the two of them went down to his car and put several boxes in the trunk. Then her dad went back over to the stairs that led up to his apartment and sat down on them. She followed and sat down next to him. That's when he turned to her and said, "Chelsea, there's something I have to tell you. Your mother really needs you. For the time being I think it would be best if you'd stay here in Meadowview. Just as soon as I get a phone, I'll call and give you my number." Chelsea felt hurt but Sam quickly soothed her when he explained, "Your mother stopped by on her way into work this morning. She really wants you to stay here with her." She had studied his face and could see the love in his eyes when he gently said, "She needs you." Suddenly Chelsea understood how deeply her father still loved her mother.

Chelsea was trying not to cry when he put his arm over her shoulders and said, "I'll be back for visits and you can visit me in Florida. Do you remember my Army buddy, Joe? He and his wife, Judy and their kids Vanessa and Vince, came up to visit us when you were nine years old."

Indeed, Sam's daughter did remember Joe and his family. Chelsea Jo Swanson had actually been named after her father's good friend. Sam Swanson and Joe Chelsea had met on an Army troop train during World War II. The two of them became enduring friends on their way to Europe. Once there, they fought side by side during the bitter cold in the Battle of the Bulge. After the war Joe had gone back home to Delite, Florida. Sam told Chelsea that in the past whenever he and Joe had been in contact, the man had always asked about his namesake.

Sam then said that he was moving to Delite and was looking forward to seeing his old friend soon. Her eyes were wide open as Chelsea asked, "How soon?" He answered, "The stores' new owner and his wife are going to be living in the apartment over the store and they don't have any furniture. There isn't going to be a moving sale after all. I'm leaving today, Chelsea."

Sam drove his daughter home and they hugged in the car. She tried to fight back the tears but just couldn't contain them. Chelsea forced herself to be strong when her dad started to cry. She said, "Daddy, don't be sad. Your life's just beginning. Be happy Daddy. You deserve it!" They hugged again, and then she got out of his car. As she had watched her father drive away that day, her sadness quickly evaporated when Chelsea's intuition kicked in and gave her the confidence to know that they would one day be reunited.

Chapter 2

Chelsea didn't like driving at night and it was beginning to get dark. With Sweetie cuddled next to her, Chelsea thought how nice it was to have the companionship of the dog. She was also thinking that her father's trip to Florida over two years ago must have been a very lonely one as she pulled into the parking lot of Miller's Motel in Spruce Pine, North Carolina. While walking toward the motel's office, Chelsea heard the mournful sound of a train horn. She turned to watch the locomotive pull its heavy load of coal and began to understand how light her own emotional burden was becoming.

After getting the key to her motel room, she drove her car across the lot. Just as she was pulling into the parking spot in front of the room, she caught a glimpse of something moving in the shadows. She slammed on the brakes and felt relieved when she saw that a person was still upright. She couldn't tell if the person was a man or woman. That's when she discovered that she had forgotten to turn on the headlights. She switched on the parking lights and got out of her car to apologize. "I'm so sorry! I forgot to put the car lights on. Are you okay?" The soft glow from the parking lights revealed a very handsome man. The smiling man said, "I admire your quick reflexes. And I'm fine thanks." Chelsea was immediately captivated by the sound of his silky, masculine voice and southern accent. She wasn't aware that her breathing had become shallow when the stranger said, "Have a nice evening." Standing frozen in place, Chelsea couldn't stop herself from staring after him. That's when she noticed that he was using a crutch and that the lower part of his left leg was missing. Chelsea got back into her car and finished parking before getting out and looking all around. When she wasn't able to spot the man anywhere, she felt very disappointed but couldn't understand why.

After putting her suitcase and Sweetie in the room, Chelsea decided to get some food. She didn't care much for bars but the one across from the motel had a food sign. The choking smell of cigarette smoke greeted her as she opened the door to the bar. She didn't notice when many heads turned to watch as she walked over to sit down at one of the tables. A waitress came over and Chelsea ordered two cheeseburgers and a large orange juice to go. While she sat waiting on her food the waitress brought her a beer. Chelsea told the waitress that she hadn't ordered a beer and the woman pointed to a disheveled looking guy standing at the bar and said it was from him. Chelsea said no thank you and asked her to please take it away. The waitress took the beer back over to the bar and said something to the guy that Chelsea couldn't hear.

On her way back to the motel room, the aroma from the cheeseburgers aroused a ravenous hunger in Chelsea. She was juggling the container of orange juice and the bag with the sandwiches while digging around in her purse for the key to her room. Being completely focused on chomping into one of the cheeseburgers, she put the key in the door and gave it a turn. It unlocked and Chelsea was just about to push open the door when she was startled by a man's gruff voice coming from behind her that said, "You really hurt my feelings when you didn't take that beer, Sweetheart." Chelsea turned toward the voice and recognized the disheveled man who had been standing at the bar. The odor of beer on his breath became overpowering as the staggering man stepped much closer.

Although Chelsea was very afraid, her sense of disgust was even stronger because of his stench. She couldn't stand the smell of beer. She had smelled it more times than she could count on Michael's breath. Trying not to give away how truly terrified she was feeling Chelsea forcefully said, "Get away from me!" The man made a grab for her, but another man stepped in between them.

The silkiness of his voice was familiar and his threatening tone was unmistakable. "The lady isn't interested. You need to leave now!" The surprised drunk swung his fist at the other man only to be met with a punch in the nose. The man stumbled backwards and fell down. That's when Chelsea saw the chance to get the door to her room open and pull her rescuer in after her. So she did it! From the window of the darkened room, she spied from behind the draperies. She watched the inebriated man struggle to get up then clumsily walk away. When she thought that he wouldn't return, she went to the bedside table and switched on the light.

She turned to see that Sweetie was sizing up their unexpected male guest. There were two large beds in the room and Chelsea watched the man who she had nearly run over earlier sit down on the one nearest to the door. It was very obvious to Chelsea that he was in pain when she saw him grimace. When he asked her for a drink of water, she quickly got it and he took a pill. The man explained that after eleven months he still occasionally needed something for pain.

Chelsea noticed a wet spot on the man's shirt and realized that some of the orange juice must have spilled on him when she pulled him into her room. She dabbed it with a face cloth while thanking him for what he had done. He volunteered that his name was James Burke. She smiled and said, "I'm Chelsea Swanson."

Sweetie began to look at the door and sound a low growl. James immediately saw a look of fear cross Chelsea's face. He softly whispered, "Turn off the light then get the dog and go into the bathroom and lock the door." Once she and Sweetie were safely in there, they heard a muffled commotion. Soon thereafter, Chelsea thought she heard a door close. Then James called out, "You can come out now, Chelsea."

She unlocked the door and timidly stepped back into the room then watched James sit down on the bed nearest to the door again. He grinned and said, "That guy decided to come back, but this time he brought one of his drunken friends with him." Then James held up his crutch and said, "So my friend and I asked them to leave!"

Chelsea giggled at his joke and opened the bag with the cheeseburgers. When she offered James one, he took it with a thank you and told her that he had just taken his first bite of a cheeseburger when he saw the drunken guy follow her out of the bar across the road. She shivered at the thought of what might have happened if James Burke hadn't decided to come after that man. James saw her shiver and told her that he would be happy to stay a little longer if she wanted. She said, "Yes! Please do!"

Sweetie loved cheeseburgers. Her constant begging was rewarded with a few bites from Chelsea's sandwich. Then James took pity on her by giving the dog some of his sandwich. Afterwards, the dog curled up on the bed where Chelsea was sitting and began to snore. Chelsea told James that the Boston Terriers' name was Sweetie and that she had belonged to her late mother. She also told him that they were moving to Florida to live with her father.

Chelsea felt safe and at ease with the man, so she naively began to talk while James propped up the pillows on the opposite bed to try and get comfortable. During the next few minutes Chelsea told him that her troubled marriage was over and that she had taken revenge on her former husband by letting him believe that she was going to remarry him. James mentally noted how quickly Chelsea admitted that she didn't feel very good about what she had done. Then he watched her yawn a few times and was surprised when he noticed that she had fallen asleep. James thought it would be fitting for him to leave the young woman's room and return to his own room in the same motel. But after some consideration, he decided to err on the side of safety and stay awhile longer in case the drunken men came back.

Sometime later Sweetie awoke and nudged the young woman next to her. Half asleep, Chelsea sat up and rubbed her eyes then wondered where she was. The sound of a male voice as he mumbled a few unintelligible words brought her fully awake. She turned on the light and could see James thrashing violently in the other bed. When she went to his side, she thought he was saying something about bears, panthers and ghosts. With his arms flailing it was a tremendous struggle for her to avoid being bashed by him. "James! James! You're having a bad dream! Wake up James! It's me Chelsea! Remember!"

James was slurring his words when he said, "You're so beautiful." Chelsea went into the bathroom to get a damp cloth. When she returned, he was sitting up and sweating profusely. Chelsea could see that his handsome face looked much older than it should have for a man of his young age. She began to dab his forehead with the dampened cloth but abruptly stopped when she looked down and saw that the palms of his hands were bleeding. James noticed her looking at his hands so he said, "I call it the creepin' crud. It's a souvenir from the jungles of Southeast Asia. I never had it until I went there."

Chelsea reached over to the nightstand and pulled a small, round tin out of her purse. She said, "I carry this salve with me all the time. It's made out of coal tar. It's good stuff." James held out his left hand but pulled it away when she touched the palm. She gently took his hand back and carefully began to massage the salve into the inside of his hand and then did the same to his right palm. By the time Chelsea finished, he told her that he thought the salve had helped.

She gave James the tin and told him to keep it. Then she said, "You were talking in your sleep. You said something about bears, panthers and ghosts." She watched James' body tense before he tersely said, "Go back to sleep Chelsea." Even though she didn't understand the change in his demeanor, she asked if he would please stay with her until the morning because she still felt afraid. He agreed to stay and Chelsea was relieved when she could hear him softly snoring. Before she nodded off, Chelsea gave thanks to God for sending James Burke at the exact moment when she had needed help.

James awoke the next morning to the unmistakable aroma of coffee and discovered that Chelsea had bought breakfast. He was enjoying the coffee and cinnamon rolls when he noticed the perplexed look on her face. She was looking at a map when she said, "How did I end up here in Spruce Pine, North Carolina? I must have taken a wrong turn in Virginia. I thought that I'd be much closer to the ocean." He was smiling when he asked, "So what was your destination if it wasn't Spruce Pine?" She replied, "The Atlantic Ocean. I've always wanted to see it, but my mother suffered from motion sickness so we didn't travel much." She pointed to a spot on the map and exclaimed, "Here! Myrtle Beach, South Carolina! This is where my best girlfriend, Andrea Chambers, and her family went for a vacation. They stayed there for two weeks between our junior and senior years of high school. I'm going to go there! Do you want to come with me?"

The animated, little girl look on her face fascinated James but he softly said, "Chelsea, the only thing you know about me is my name." She smiled at him and said, "I also know that I like

17

you and trust you James Burke." He thought for a few moments then said, "Okay. I'll go."

Sweetie had been begging but hadn't received even one bite. James saw that Chelsea wasn't going to eat the last little bit of her sweet roll so he gave it to the very grateful dog. James was astonished when the little bug-eyed creature didn't even take time to chew the morsel, but instead swallowed it whole. The little dog snorted excitedly and Chelsea said, "From now on, she'll expect you to give her a bite of your people food every time you eat."

Chelsea packed her car while James returned to his room for a quick shower. He came out of his room just in time to see Chelsea trying to lock the door to her room while struggling to control the dog. Sweetie was tugging so hard on her leash that Chelsea couldn't even get the key into the lock. James took the leash and went to the passenger side of the front seat. The eager dog jumped in first so Chelsea warned James to turn his face away before he got in the car or he would have a wet tongue all over it.

They drove over to the motel's office and settled their bills with the clerk then James asked where he could turn in his bus ticket. It didn't take long for him to take care of that and they were soon on their way to Myrtle Beach, South Carolina.

They hadn't gone far when James politely pointed out to Chelsea that she had missed a turn. After he guided her back to the correct road he discretely picked up the map and diplomatically said, "Perhaps I'll take care of the map reading so that you won't have to be bothered with it." Chelsea giggled and said, "James, you think I'm going to make another wrong turn like I did in Virginia." He merely looked at her and smiled. Chelsea had heard that southern gentlemen are very well mannered, and it was certainly true of James Burke.

With some miles between them and Spruce Pine, North Carolina, Chelsea noticed that James was constantly switching positions and appeared to look uncomfortable. Soon she stopped for some gas and to exercise Sweetie.

After Chelsea paid for the gas, she put the dog back in the car then drove across the road to an ice cream stand. James said that he didn't want anything, but Chelsea bought him a soda pop anyway and returned with a vanilla sugar cone for herself. It didn't go unnoticed by Sweetie that food was on its way. James quickly grabbed the dog's leash to keep her from completely vaulting out through the open window. Chelsea gently pulled Sweetie through the front passenger window then opened the back passenger door and sat down on the backseat. She ate most of the ice cream while holding onto the dog's leash. Chelsea then gave the dog what was left. Sweetie wolfed down the cold snack so fast that it caused Chelsea to wonder if it gave the animal a headache.

Out of the corner of her eye Chelsea saw James take one of his pain pills along with a swig of the soda pop. After he did that, she took the boxes that were sitting on the backseat and put them next to the sewing machine in the rear of her station wagon. She covered the backseat with a sheet and several pillows. Then Chelsea suggested to James that he might be more comfortable if he could stretch out in the backseat. He didn't hesitate to get back there. Right then the dog began to cough. The two humans thought Sweetie was going to upchuck the ice cream cone, but she didn't. That episode caused James to remark, "I hope that the people food diet isn't making Little Bug-Eyes sick."

After James had crawled into the backseat he felt a lump under him. He pulled out a lavender teddy bear with bright yellow, glass button eyes and asked, "What's this?" Chelsea replied, "That's Teddy! My daddy gave him to me!" Her reference to her father as being, "my daddy," revealed Chelsea's naturally sweet and innocent nature. That brought a smile to James' face.

They had traveled for about thirty minutes when James said, "I'm feeling a lot better. The cramping has stopped." That's when Chelsea realized that she had somehow managed to head north instead of Southeast. She was thinking of telling James about her blunder in the exact moment he noticed that she was going the wrong way. He reached for the map and said, "I believe we're headed in the wrong direction. We'll be back on track soon." A short time later Chelsea felt grateful that he had guided her in the right direction. She silently thanked God again for sending James Burke into her life.

Some hours later James said, "Smell that Chelsea? It's the ocean." James and Chelsea felt weary, but the dog was a fountain of energy. Sweetie stuck her head out of the passenger window and excitedly sniffed the air. As they drove on a road close to the beach, Chelsea and James began to feel invigorated. Chelsea said, "The air is so fresh here." When James pointed to a motel with a no vacancy sign, Chelsea could hardly wait for them to get checked into their rooms so that she could walk down to the water's edge.

She quickly put her things into her room then Chelsea and Sweetie began to walk toward the beach. James' room was right next to Chelsea's. He saw them walking toward the beach and followed. He watched as Chelsea seemed to bounce with each step that she took, and he secretly wished that he wasn't so willing to admire the loveliness of her.

Chelsea became enthralled with the ocean view and missed the sign that read, NO DOGS ALLOWED. James caught up with her and pointed to the sign. Chelsea picked up the disappointed dog and took her back to their motel room. With a bribe of a few doggy treats from Chelsea, Sweetie was much more agreeable to being left alone.

As she walked back toward the beach, Chelsea could see James' blond hair being tossed by the ocean breezes. That gentle movement caused him to appear even more handsome. She had no way of knowing that he was smiling at the thought of her and her dog when she said, "I'm back."

The two of them watched the waves lap the shore as they slowly moved closer to the water. Chelsea bent down and stuck her finger into the frothy liquid then tasted it. James was amazed when she seemed surprised as she said, "It really does taste salty! My friend Andrea said that it would!"

James pointed toward the eastern horizon and said, "Look Chelsea. There's a thunderstorm out at sea." As the two of them watched the lightning dash across the sky, neither realized that they were cuddling. Finally aware of their close contact, James gently moved away from Chelsea. Then he suggested that they should get some dinner. Although Chelsea was reluctant to leave the enchanted world that she had discovered, she managed to tear herself away.

They bought some seafood take-out dinners and returned to the motel. Chelsea invited James into her room by saying, "There's no reason for us to eat alone." The dog greeted them as soon as they opened the door. As usual she was ready for a snack. All through dinner Sweetie entertained them with her antics as she begged for some small bites.

Chelsea was genuinely interested when James told her that on numerous occasions his father and he had gone deep-sea fishing with friends in the Atlantic Ocean and the Gulf of Mexico. James was honestly amused when Chelsea told him that before she left Myrtle Beach, she wanted to play tag with the ocean waves just like her friend Andrea Chambers and her family had done when they vacationed there. After they finished eating, the two of them agreed to meet on the following morning at seven thirty.

Sweetie was already curled up on the bed when Chelsea got out of the shower. Chelsea towel dried her hair and realized that for the first time in a long time she actually felt happy. When she crawled into bed, she had no doubt that her sleep would be pleasant and filled with peaceful dreams. Although James was exhausted, he knew that he would put in another restless night filled with haunting memories and disturbing images.

Chapter 3

Chelsea awoke feeling alive and refreshed. She had no way of knowing that James had been wrestling with his unwelcome yet familiar nightly visitors. Even though the face of the dark-haired beauty and her dog had momentarily appeared in his dreams to comfort and console him, James was engulfed in fatigue.

They met outside their rooms by Chelsea's vehicle and decided to get some breakfast. Chelsea took her dog hoping to find a restaurant with a window so that she could keep an eye on her. Later while James and Chelsea were eating, they had to laugh when they saw Sweetie jump onto the car's dashboard. Even though the dog had already eaten, Chelsea saved a small piece of toast for her anyway. When they got back to the car, the dog's entire body seemed to be wagging when she was given the tiny treat.

They returned to the motel and Chelsea took Sweetie for a short walk. When they got back, they found James standing next to his suitcase outside the door to Sweetie and Chelsea's room. He picked up his suitcase and the three of them went into the room. When Chelsea took off Sweetie's leash, the dog immediately ran to her water dish and began to lap the liquid. Chelsea was watching her dog and didn't see that James had opened the curtain on the front window. She finally looked up and noticed that he seemed to be deep in thought. Chelsea was completely caught off guard when he said in a soft voice, "I'm married, Chelsea. I should have told you two nights ago. I apologize for not doing that." James turned to look at her. As he searched her face for a reaction he said, "I didn't mean to..." Chelsea interrupted. "James, you've done nothing wrong. I consider myself fortunate to have met you. You came to my aid that first night. You're a gentleman and you don't need to apologize." He smiled when she said that. Then the two of them went down to the shore one last time so that she could play tag with the waves. After that she drove him to a nearby bus station and they went their separate ways.

James waited for thirty minutes before the bus arrived. During the trip, he dozed intermittently. He awoke in a state of drowsiness when the bus slowed down while entering the small town of Coshville, Georgia. When he turned to look out the window, his eyes were drawn to the steamy sight along the side of the street. He cried out, "Stop the bus! Please!" James was already standing when the driver pulled over. "Is there a problem sir?" asked the concerned driver. James replied, "Everything's fine. I just need to get off here."

While James was walking toward what he had seen, he could hear a man saying, "It'll be awhile. We'll get that thermostat and put it in for you." Her satiny voice said, "My dog needs to get out of this hot sun. Do you know a place where we can go?" The man pointed to a large group of trees across the street and told her that she would find a restaurant with an outdoor covered patio on the other side of the town square. Sweetie became excited when she saw James and almost jumped out of Chelsea's arms. James asked, "Mind if I put my suitcase in your car?" Chelsea whirled around at the sound of his voice and exclaimed, "James!

The dog and the two humans walked through the trees in the town square. James and Chelsea were amused by Sweetie as she jumped and snorted each time she saw a bird. They came upon a pavilion that was hidden by huge tall oaks. The shade from the trees caused the structure to feel like an oasis as the oaks cooled it and the old stone walkway which surrounded the pavilion. The two them were tempted to linger there but their hunger spurred them on.

They followed a well-worn dirt path lined with more trees and park benches until they stepped out of the shade and into the bright sunshine. There they were amazed to find a tall bronze statue of a Confederate soldier. The soldier stood motionless keeping watch towards the north. It seemed as though his eyes could penetrate his present day realm while he waited for an unseen enemy to move. James looked up at the statue and Chelsea watched his body tense. Then she noticed that his breathing had become shallow. She gently touched his arm and that seemed to draw him away from wherever his mind had taken him.

They crossed the street and went to the restaurant with the covered patio. James sat down at a picnic table right across from Chelsea. He watched her tie her dog's leash to one of the table's legs. Then he saw Chelsea look up when a young waitress came to take their food orders. Against his better judgment, James ordered an extra chilidog for Little Bug-Eyes. He knew that she shouldn't be given spicy people food, but he'd grown attached to the dog and found it difficult to resist her begging.

James wasn't really listening to Chelsea's chatter, but he thought he heard her say something about all the steam that had come out from underneath the hood of her car. Then he saw and heard the restaurant's kitchen screen door slam shut. Suddenly, his senses began to reel. He tried desperately to control his mind, but his thinking became scattered. Nightmarish memories of the day when his best friend, Kevin Scoggins, died came charging through his thoughts. Then James felt a strong breeze on his face. He watched a large man in a white apron prop the kitchen door of the restaurant open. The man then turned around and went back into the kitchen. That's when James saw the blades of the kitchen's ceiling fan slowly spinning. Below the fan, a woman was rolling pie dough and sprinkling flour while the white dust began to billow in the air.

James turned his head and looked out toward the street. He saw two young boys walking by. They were eating big red apples. He watched them until they went out of his sight. Then he felt compelled to look back toward the statue of the silent soldier that was standing guard in the town square. A beam of sunlight pierced through the patio's canopy and fell across James' eyes. Dizziness overwhelmed him. Chelsea stopped in mid sentence when she heard an elderly gentlemen sitting next to them ask, "Son, are you alright?"

By the time Chelsea rose from the picnic bench and ran around to James, he had already fallen onto the cement floor of the patio. He was soaked in perspiration and bleeding from a cut above his right eyebrow. The large man wearing a white apron hurried out of the kitchen and put a towel under James' head. Then the waitress gave Chelsea a cloth filled with ice. Chelsea realized that James was coming to when he flinched as she touched the cut above his eye with the cold cloth. He tried to get up but the large man in the apron gently held him down and said, "You need to lay here for awhile, Buddy." After a few minutes

James sat up and insisted that he was going to be fine. Chelsea said that she wanted to take him to a doctor, but he became defensive so she didn't press the point. The waitress soon brought their food order and they paid for it. Then James said that he wanted to go back to the shaded pavilion area of the park square to eat.

The pavilion seemed to welcome them when they sat down on one of the benches within it. James still looked extremely weary but the color was back in his face. Chelsea noticed that he was sipping his lemon blend, but that he hadn't taken a bite of food. She couldn't eat much either because of her concern for James and only gave Sweetie a few bites of the spicy chilidog. What was left got tossed into a trashcan. Then they all went to get her car.

The mechanic assured her that the car was in good working order when she paid him. Soon they were once again on their way. James seemed to be resting comfortably in the backseat and Chelsea didn't want to bother him with giving her directions. She decided that she could be sure that she was driving south for the rest of the afternoon if she just made certain that the sun was on her right side. As the day wound down, James' appearance and mood was much improved.

Chelsea found a motel close to a diner. When she checked in, she requested a room with two beds. James resisted sharing a room with her but agreed to it when he began to feel woozy. Once she got him and her dog situated in their room, she went to get some food. While waiting for the food she spotted a drug store. She returned to the motel room with the food and an antibacterial spray.

James was really tempted when Chelsea let him see and smell the baked chicken, mashed potatoes, mixed vegetables and rolls. Then she told him that he wasn't going to get even one bite of it unless he agreed to have the cut above his eye cleaned and treated with the spray. James made her laugh when he joked about how she wanted to torture him before she fed him.

During dinner Sweetie went into her half-starved act and was rewarded with several bites of chicken. She finally realized that she wasn't going to get any more people food when James went to his bed and laid down. The dog ran to her dish and slurped down some water before running and jumping up onto James' bed where she made herself comfortable right next to him.

Chelsea cleaned the table before sitting down on her bed across from James. She said, "I know that you probably don't want to talk about it, but I have to tell you that I was very afraid for you when you fell earlier today." James shook his head and said, "I suppose I owe you an explanation. What happened involves my best friend, Kevin Scoggins." After he took a deep breath James said, "We met at school when we were in the first grade. From then on we did everything together. Kevin was the finest baseball player that I've ever personally known. In high school he was really good looking and the girls gave him the nickname, Face. When we wanted to meet girls, we'd send Kev out in front of us and he'd draw them in like a magnet.

After we graduated from high school, my dad helped both of us find work at a construction company. We built wooden frames for houses. He was my best man when I got married. We both thought that we were going to be drafted so we joined the Army together. We went to Ft. Leonard Wood in Missouri for our boot camp and training. We even went to South Vietnam together." Then James choked out, "But we didn't die together."

Chelsea inhaled sharply and her heart went out to James. He was crying and she wanted to comfort him but wasn't sure how to do it. Tears tried to force themselves from her own eyes, but she fought to hold them back for his sake. When she suggested to him that he might feel better if he took a shower, he agreed. The sound of the falling water as he showered produced a great sadness in Chelsea. A deluge of tears soon began. Later she managed to hide her red swollen eyes from James by pretending to be asleep.

Chelsea had somehow managed to actually fall asleep but was awakened when a car engine outside their room revved loudly. Sweetie jumped down to get a drink of water and James sat up on his bed. Chelsea asked, "Did you hear that loud car?" He answered, "Yes." Thinking out loud she said, "Michael had a loud car until he wrecked it. Then he bought a loud pick-up truck and wrecked it." James chuckled and said, "Your ex-husband sounds like a poor driver." She replied, "No. He was a very good driver when he wasn't drinking. And he did that almost everyday. He always had plenty of money for his beer and another woman, but he seldom helped out with the rent and groceries." Chelsea then told James that she probably sounded like a harpy. He politely told her that she didn't. After she told him that she really wanted to let go of all the anger that she was feeling, he said that he thought it would be awhile before that could happen.

Chelsea kept talking while James sat on his bed and politely listened even though he only wanted to close his eyes and go back to sleep. She told him that Michael had been a customer at the bank where she worked as a teller. She said, "He would show up at my window even when he didn't have any banking business to do. We dated for three months before he proposed. My mother said that she didn't trust him and told me not to marry him." Chelsea sighed while shaking her head and said, "I wish I had listened to Mother."

She told James about all the times Michael said that he had to work late or needed to leave town for the weekend because of his job. Then one night he came home drunk and said that he was leaving her so he could live with another woman. By that time, Chelsea said that she had become thoroughly fed up with how he was treating her so she told him that she didn't care where he lived. The next day she consulted with a divorce attorney. Chelsea said, "Two weeks later the other woman Michael was living with came to my apartment crying. She said that Michael was drinking a lot and that she had caught him with another woman. She didn't get any sympathy from me!"

Chelsea paused briefly and James thought she looked so sad before she finally said, "The day after that woman came to my apartment, I was feeling ill. I went into work anyway, but before noon I got very sick to my stomach. I really thought that I was going to vomit. My mother and the bank's manager told me to go home. I was just about to get into my car and leave when Michael showed up. He kept insisting that I shouldn't get a divorce and that he wanted me to take him back. He wouldn't let go of my arm! Then my stomach did a flip-flop and I threw up all over his shoes!" James couldn't keep from laughing even though he could tell that Chelsea was feeling a little embarrassed by what had happened.

Chelsea felt her mood lighten a bit because of the sound of his laughter. She continued. "On the day of the divorce trial Michael told the judge that he didn't want a divorce, but I said that I did. When the judge asked me why, I told him that I no longer trusted Michael and that I didn't want to remain in a marriage with him. My lawyer later told me that he saw a look of disbelief on Michael's face when I said that." Chelsea paused briefly then said, "I can't understand how Michael could possibly think that I still trusted him after everything he did. And how can I feel such regret, sadness and anger all at the same time?" Then Chelsea asked in a soft voice, "And why do I still love him?" Her mixed emotions touched James because he could relate to them.

Chelsea didn't expect to hear James say, "My wife had an affair while I was overseas. She broke it off when she found out that I had been wounded." James looked thoughtful and said, "I'm partly to blame because I decided to join the Army without including her in that decision. Margot said that she felt as though she had been abandoned. She told me the affair is over and asked me to forgive her." James looked straight into Chelsea's eyes and said, "I'm going to try very hard to do that." Chelsea could see that James genuinely meant what he said, so she silently prayed that God would give him a forgiving heart. Then she felt grieved by her own lack of forgiveness toward Michael.

James watched a tear roll down her cheek when Chelsea said, "Michael never asked for my forgiveness and I wonder if he even realizes that his actions are what caused our divorce. I'm certain that his family has something to do with his behavior. I've never been able to figure them out. I never once saw them being nice to each other. It was as though they were in a competition to see who could be the meanest. And I guess I won that contest!" Chelsea looked troubled by that realization.

James was puzzled. He found it hard to believe that Chelsea Swanson had a mean bone in her body. He asked, "Why do you think you won the *who can be the meanest* contest?" James saw another tear slowly fall down her cheek when she told him that she had hung a mean sign on the bedroom wall that read,

TOUCHED YOU LAST. Then Chelsea reminded him that she had let Michael think that she was going to remarry him. James thought for a moment then softly said, "So you left him standing at the alter. After what he did to you, he had it coming."

Chelsea felt drained of her strength physically and emotionally. She had cried more times than she could count over the past year and couldn't imagine from where tonight's tears had come. And she was somewhat upset with herself because she couldn't annihilate all of the negative feelings that she was carrying. She even secretly wondered if she had gotten so used to thinking in such an undesirable way that it had now become ingrained in her. Chelsea finally realized that she shouldn't keep wrestling with such adverse feelings and she began to pray that God would fill her mind with goodness and instill His spirit of forgiveness in her heart. When she did that His presence seemed to wrap around her and she drifted off to sleep.

During the wee hours of the morning, Sweetie jumped onto the bed where Chelsea was sleeping and began to paw at her arm. Chelsea heard James cry out in his sleep so she went to awaken him from his nightmare. Her soft voice and gentle touch pulled him away from the fierceness of his dreams and brought him into the stillness of the early morning. Chelsea remembered how James had reacted on that first night, but she decided to tell him anyway that he'd been talking in his sleep about bears, panthers and ghosts again. Then she said, "James, perhaps it would help you if you told me about your bad dreams."

Chapter 4

Chelsea went into the bathroom and came back with a damp facecloth. She gently placed it on James' forehead then sat down on the edge of her bed and looked at him. James looked into her eyes and asked, "Are you sure you want to hear this?" She told him that she did as she patted the little dog by her side.

He said, "Before Kevin and I arrived in Vietnam we didn't know what to expect. One of the sergeants passed out ten bullets to each man. Now this didn't seem to be near enough to some of us, but the staff sergeant assured us that the amount of ammunition he had given to us was sufficient to carry on a small war. His words weren't comforting. But after we arrived, nothing happened. We were assigned to a base, and for the first month it was just plain boring.

On the morning of the first of October 1967, our platoon sergeant asked Kevin and me if we wanted to go on a helicopter ride to take some supplies to a forward base. We jumped at the chance. We were sent to a supply sergeant and he told us to help load the chopper. We helped the crew put on bags of mail, powdered eggs, powdered chocolate milk, flour and cardboard boxes filled with apples. The supply sergeant saw us eying the apples. Since this was a delicacy that we hadn't had for a while, he told us that we could each have one of the shiny red treats, but only one.

It was a bright, sunny day and we'd been in the air for about thirty minutes. We noticed puffs of flour and wondered why there was so much of the white dust in the air. Then we realized that we were being fired on. The helicopter started flying erratically, and the sound became deafening. I looked at Kevin and he was looking at me. I closed my eyes, held my M-16 tightly and prayed.

The next thing I knew, I was lying on the ground with the wind knocked out of me. I turned my head toward the wreckage and saw a few yards away that Kevin was also on the ground. I realized immediately that he was dead. As I regained my breath, I saw the two crewmembers. They were also dead. In the distance, I could hear excited voices yelling in Vietnamese. Then I heard a voice say in English, 'Can you walk? Can you walk? Hurry! Charley's coming! They'll capture you!' The man spoke with a familiar accent. It sounded like my mother's cousins who live in one of the parishes near New Orleans.

I rolled over and looked at Kevin, then grabbed by weapon. I went toward the two men standing nearby. One of the men had a tattoo of a Confederate flag on his forearm. He spoke with a southern accent, but I couldn't tell where he was from. They told me to follow them into the jungle. That's when I saw that there was a column of men ahead of them. I can't recall much about the first day, except that we walked almost constantly. I thought about Kevin, my parents, my wife and home.

We stopped briefly, and the man the others called Ghost told me to give him my dog tags, wallet and wedding ring. I didn't want to do that, but he insisted. He told me, 'If Charley captures you, they could possibly use them against you.' Then the man called Bear cut out part of a map with his knife. The map was plastic like a plastic tablecloth. He took my belongings, wrapped them in the piece of map, slit the earth open with his knife and pushed the small bundle into the opening. With one move of his foot, he closed the ground. He then notched a nearby tree with his knife once near the ground and again a few feet above that. We walked until the light started to fade and then we rested for the night. They shared their rations with me.

The next morning our journey began early. We followed a path until the hills became steeper. Eventually we were into the small mountains. Having grown up in Florida, I wasn't used to such steep terrain. Ft. Leonard Wood had hills, but they were not as steep or as large as these were. We tried to walk on the sides of the hills. Occasionally, we needed to cross a ridgeline. We tried to stay away from the valley floors. My legs were sore and I thought that I wouldn't be able to continue. A man they called Beer Keg said, 'It helps to have been raised in hill country.' The one they called Panther smiled and told me to, 'Think about drinking a cold six-pack of beer, and you'll forget about your sore legs.' That's when I realized that Panther was the man that I saw at the crash site who sounded like he might have been from one of the parishes near New Orleans. I said, 'I'd rather think about eating a nice piece of Key Lime pie.' They referred to me as Key Lime after that.

The men in the column were silent most of the time. I began to notice that their uniforms were a bit different from mine. They had no designation of rank and there were no emblems. None of the men appeared to have dog tags. Even their boots were different from mine. My boots left a distinctive tread mark. Their boots left what looked like an imprint of a sandal. Each man was armed with a forty-five-caliber pistol. They each carried two canteens on their belt. Out of necessity I had to adapt to their ways. They operated differently from the way I had been trained. It was apparent that they were familiar with the surrounding territory.

As we traveled, we encountered several fresh water springs. They refilled some of the canteens and put water purification tablets in them. They told me that even though the water tasted fine, it probably contained bacteria that might be harmful. As the light faded, we once again rested for the night.

The man called Missoula offered me a drink from his second canteen. It contained tequila. I'm not sure what tequila tastes like out of a glass bottle, but out of a metal canteen it tastes just terrible. A number of the men had alcohol in their second canteen. The men were more talkative that night. I asked if they were Marines, but I didn't believe that they were. Ghost answered, 'No. We're part of a Naval unit.' They told me that we were in North Vietnam. I wasn't entirely surprised because we had been walking in a northerly direction.

I remember everything about the second day. I can recall all of what I saw and did, including every step I took. We were up at dawn. After we ate our rations, we were to break off into two groups. I was to go with the smaller group. Bear said that we were headed to an area that should not have much activity. The largest group was going to head east. My group was to head north. As the two groups separated, the men made a low quacking sound. It was a most peculiar sight to see grown men quacking."

Chelsea asked, "James, do you know why they were quacking?" He replied, "No, but I believe it was a sign of respect because all of the men seemed very serious as none were smiling." Then she asked, "Did you ever see the group that went east again?" "No." he said. "That morning we traveled to an area where there were many walking trails. We started to see villages and some open fields. The houses were neat and spaced side by side to form an oval. There was a courtyard at the center of each village. In the smallest villages the houses formed a circle.

Before noon, from the hillside we spotted the enemy in the distance. They were grouped up and were resting in the shade of trees. They had bicycles packed with supplies. Missoula called in an air strike. Then about five minutes later, a low flying aircraft dropped its deadly load. Moments later a second aircraft added to the destruction.

We waited for a short while, then the man they called Kameha told me to follow him to the strike area. We cautiously descended the hill. When we neared the bombed area, Kameha searched through the debris for a usable canvas tarp. I gratefully took it because I was without rain gear. I noticed a dead Vietnamese man. On the ground near to him was a photograph of a group of young women. They were all dressed in dark colors and wearing rice hats. I wondered if one of them was his wife or perhaps a girlfriend. Kameha picked up a package that was about the size of a cracker box. We took no personal items from the dead, because if we were captured we could receive harsh treatment if these items were to be found on us.

We returned to our companions and then traveled west for an hour. During the late afternoon, we came to some high ground. From that vantage point we were able to see a long narrow valley. We were near the south end. At the north end, there was a village. A trail and a small stream ran through the middle of the valley. There were numerous vegetable plots and small fields. I saw something orange in one field and wondered if it was some type of squash. Bear said to me, 'Do you see those two water buffalo looking up at us?' I nodded and Bear said, 'They know that we're here. They'll lose interest in awhile.' The two animals were staring right up at our exact position! Bear said, 'If the enemy should start to come through, the water buffalo will know it before we do.'

Ghost told me how the enemy moved their supplies. They pushed bicycles carrying supplies to the south and west. Many different trails were used to supply Charley in the south. Empty bicycles went north and east. When the bicycles weren't loaded, they would sit on them and coast down hill and that it was impressive to see so many of them in a row. They moved quite rapidly. Bear said, 'When we call a strike, we usually call it on the loaded bicycles. But sometimes we have to call it on the empty bicycles. There are times when we have to call a strike near a village when there is no traffic on a trail. It has to appear random. The pilots may not attack our target. They may find a better target such as a column of trucks. It depends on who is in the air. We're low priority.'

I could see that Kameha had an impish grin. He was opening the package that he had earlier taken from the strike area. It was individually wrapped candy bars with some kind of oriental writing on them. Bear joked that maybe it was Chinese laxative. We all devoured that candy. The wrappers were buried in the ground.

At dusk we could hear laughter coming from the village. Kameha said, 'I'll call out for supper tonight. Let's have chicken, mashed potatoes and biscuits with honey.' Missoula said, 'Don't cook tonight! Call Chicken Delight!' We all had a hushed laugh. I could see that for a few brief moments their thoughts were drawn away from the task at hand. Perhaps they were thinking of home as I was.

The next morning the water buffalo were looking toward the village. We thought that perhaps a farmer was coming to feed them. Instead, it was a column of loaded bicycles being pushed south. We waited until they had passed by. Then a strike was called in. Before the planes arrived, another column came out of the village. There may have been a hundred men. They weren't pushing bicycles. Someone said that they were North Vietnamese Army regulars. They had moved directly below our position by the time the first plane struck the bicycle pushers. Then a second plane also attacked the bicycle column. The regular soldiers scattered and some took cover near our position. We stayed as low to the ground as we could. We didn't dare to move. I heard a sound and wondered for a while what it was. I soon realized that it was my own heartbeat. The regulars stayed off the trail for nearly a half hour. We heard someone yell orders and they returned to the valley. The regulars moved south and we went north. No one knew why the regulars were there. We thought perhaps that one of our pilots had been shot down.

For the next three weeks we moved in different directions. At times we retraced our steps or crisscrossed the trails that we had previously traveled. We called one or more air strikes on regular army units. Each day more and more regulars headed south.

Early one morning we started to walk south. On the morning of the third day, Missoula called command. Everything was said in code. We waited for a couple of hours and then we moved south. We walked for about five miles. I could see a village off to our right. There was a road beyond the field in front of us. Along the edge of the road there was a long row of large trees. We started to cross the field in front of us going toward the trees. The next thing that I can remember is, I was in a field hospital. The doctor there told me that I had lost my left leg just below the knee. Shortly after that I was sent to a base hospital. They operated on my leg and took a piece of metal out of my left shoulder. At the hospital, the doctors asked me my name. They weren't sure I was who I said I was.

A week later I was sent to a hospital in Japan. I was again questioned by some officers. I told them what I've been telling you. Then I was flown to Hawaii and taken to the Tripler Army Hospital. There they put me in a wheel chair and a medic pushed me to a private room. The medic said, 'You must be a very important guy. These rooms are reserved for generals and admirals when they have their bunions removed.'

A doctor and two nurses checked my wounds and changed my bandages. After they left, two Army officers entered the room and shut the door behind them. They introduced themselves as Lt. Gray and Captain O'Neil. They told me that I'd been missing for thirty days. Then they told me to tell them my story while they tape-recorded me. During the next four days, they returned and would briefly question me. The hospital staff treated me very well. Several of the nurses privately told me that they were not allowed to talk to me about the war.

Sometime later a man named Captain Kohler came to my room. He was a most unmilitary looking man. It seemed to me that he would be more suited to driving a tractor or trapping muskrats. He certainly had no military bearing. Captain Kohler asked me what I could remember about the time I'd been missing. He also asked me if I could tell him the given surnames of the men that I'd been with during those thirty days. I told him that I hadn't heard their given surnames. Then he asked me which of the men was in charge. I told him that I didn't know. Captain Kohler said, 'In any given unit it would soon become apparent who was in charge.' I told him that it appeared to me that they all went about their tasks as if it was second nature to them.

Then the captain said, 'The United States has no ground forces operating in North Vietnam.' He then asked me if I'd gone AWOL for the month. Of course I said, no! He asked if I thought I might have been captured. Then he said, 'Sometimes Charley will take prisoners then release them after a short time.' Captain Kohler then asked me if I'd gone over to the communist side. I told him that I was neither captured nor a traitor, but that I couldn't vouch for my missing leg. When I said that, he laughed. Then he told me that I would soon be fitted for a prosthetic leg. After that I'd be interviewed by a psychiatrist.

I received the leg and went through therapy. I was allowed to walk outside of the building on the hospital grounds. I met with the psychiatrist on numerous occasions. He had me draw lots of pictures. I drew houses, flowers and outdoor scenes. I became fairly good at it and for a while I thought about attending art school.

One day Captain Kohler came to see me. He told me again that we have no ground forces in North Vietnam. He said that he had been told by various doctors that when someone had gone through traumatic events, that it was possible for the mind to create a false history. He said to me, 'You saw your buddy killed that day. Your mind may have been trying to protect you. When you needed help, there were men right there. They were familiar with the territory that you traveled through. They knew where the springs of water were, and they shared their rations with you. Almost every day you came close to the enemy, yet you were

36

never discovered. Can you remember being wounded?' I told him that I had tried to remember that, but I just couldn't.

Before Captain Kohler left me, I asked him how many enlisted men in Tripler Hospital were in a private room? He said, 'There have been enlisted men in private rooms who have been very badly wounded.'

I was supplied with new uniforms as my old ones never caught up with me. I was awarded a Purple Heart and received a promotion to private first class while I was still in the hospital.

Captain Kohler came in early one morning and said that he'd located a marine that had been wounded at Tam Da on the same day that I was. He told me to, 'Get dressed. We're going for a short ride. The marine is assigned to CINCPAC. I've made arrangements for us to speak with him.'

I enjoyed the morning. I'd been cooped up at the hospital for a while and it felt good to have a change of scenery. As we drove up the blacktopped driveway that led to CINCPAC, I was impressed by all the vegetation. The various colors and fragrances of the flowers still come to the forefront of my mind.

At CINCPAC we were escorted to a briefing room. There we met with Navy Commander Lake, Petty Officer James and Corporal Cooper. Commander Lake's uniform displayed the wings of a Navy pilot. James was an older gentleman. Cooper was about my age. I noticed that on his uniform, Cooper wore a Purple Heart. Captain Kohler spoke to Commander Lake and expressed his desire to ask Corporal Cooper about what happened at Tam Da on the 30th of October 1967.

Commander Lake said, 'The report on Tam Da is classified, however, within the report are some sections that remain unclassified. If the conversation enters an area that's classified, that exchange will be interrupted.' Kohler asked Corporal Cooper if he recognized me. Cooper said he didn't. Kohler told them that I was wounded when the truck that I was riding in hit a mine near Tam Da. Cooper said, 'We picked up a soldier that day, but the man was much thinner than Burke here. His face hadn't seen a razor for some time.' Kohler then asked Cooper if he could give us the names of some of the other

Marines that were with him that day. Petty Officer James interrupted and said, 'It is best if that information is not released.'

Kohler then asked Cooper to describe what had happened on the 30th of October 1967. Cooper said, 'That morning we were ordered to take two days rations. We were told that we were going to make a sweep near Tam Da. Usually we were flown in but on that day our company took four, two and a half ton trucks. I rode in the fourth truck. There are several villages named Tam Da. We were going to the northern most one. We stopped before we got to Tam Da. We could see the village and it was about a mile away. There was a long line of trees beside the road. Also, farm fields were on both sides of the road. Behind the trees to the south of the road, there were some villagers working in one of the fields. They were women and children. Our lieutenant told us to stay in the trucks. The lieutenant walked toward the first truck and he was looking at the village. We began to get nervous because we were just sitting out there in the open. Charley had been active in that area and there was thick, brushy foliage beyond the fields.

Our captain had been riding in the first truck, so I assumed that the lieutenant was going to talk to him. A few minutes later he returned with a soldier. He helped the soldier get into the back of our truck. Then the trucks were turned around in the road. That put our truck at the front of the column.

We headed back toward the base. After we had gone about two miles, we hit a land mine. Our lieutenant and the driver were killed. I received a foot wound.' Captain Kohler then asked, 'Was the soldier who got in your truck armed?' Cooper said, 'He had an M-16.' Kohler also asked if Cooper had seen anyone else at the spot where the Marine company had picked up the soldier. Cooper said that he hadn't seen anyone else. Kohler asked if their company had ever before gone out to make a sweep but then had not been deployed to the field. Cooper said, 'No.' The interview had not answered many questions with regards to the 30th of October in 1967.

Before returning to the hospital, Captain Kohler and I went for a ride through Honolulu, then on to Waikiki. We drove near a large tank that looked like a pineapple. Captain Kohler said, 'It holds water not pineapple juice.' We saw a statue of King

Kamehameha. We also saw the new state capital building. At Waikiki, we drove along the beach for a while. We stopped and bought ice cream cones. There was a sign in the window that said PRESIDENT JOHNSON ATE ICE CREAM HERE! I looked over at Diamond Head and watched all the people on the beach. They were all having a good time, but my life was forever changed. Captain Kohler drove me back to Tripler and I thanked him for the tour.

Before he left me he asked, 'Do you remember when you got into the truck with those Marines, and do you remember the explosion from the land mine?' My answer to both questions was no.

Captain Kohler was later transferred to the Pentagon. About a week before I was released from the hospital, I awoke one morning and found a large envelope on my bedside table. It contained a smaller envelope that held my wedding ring, my wallet and my dog tags. There was no return address on the envelope. The postmark was Travis Air Force Base in California. Previously, all of the mail I received while I was hospitalized was addressed to Private First Class James Burke. This envelope just had my name on it with no designation of rank." James looked thoughtful and said, "I was in Vietnam for three months. I was in a helicopter that was shot down. I was in a truck that was blown up. I lost my best friend and I lost my leg. I never fired my weapon at the enemy, not one time."

At the conclusion of the strange account, James looked bewildered and Chelsea realized that what he had lived through could easily overwhelm anyone. Although she wondered if he would ever be able to recover the lost memories, Chelsea knew for certain that James Burke was a man who could deal with anything that life would throw at him.

Chapter 5

Because it was almost dawn Chelsea and James decided to get cleaned up and check out of the motel. Since James already knew that Chelsea was going to Florida he asked her if it would be possible for her to take him to Lakeland. She told him that Lakeland was right on her way. Although neither of them said so, they both realized that this would probably be their last day together and they wouldn't see each other ever again.

Their early start had been advantageous because they arrived in Lakeland well before noon. They had shared coffee and donuts while traveling and stopped only briefly to get gas and exercise Sweetie. When James spotted a phone booth, he asked Chelsea to stop so he could get directions to the nearest bus station. While driving him to that bus station, Chelsea was tempted to ask him where his home was located even though she understood how wrong it would be for her to know. When they arrived, he could see tears welling up in her eyes. He wiped them away with his thumb and said, "It's best that it ends this way Chelsea. I want you to drive away now and don't look back." Then he patted the dog on her head and got out of the car. Although Chelsea didn't want to, she did what he told her to do and resisted taking one last look in her rear view mirror as she drove down the street. James watched her car drive out of his sight, and then he walked into the bus station.

During the afternoon, Chelsea's thoughts were of James. The distraction caused her to almost miss the turn off to Delite. Sweetie perked up when Chelsea said, "We'll be there soon. It will be good to see my daddy again."

Because Sam Swanson knew his daughter's sense of direction was less than perfect, he had given her very precise directions to the mobile home park and told her exactly how to get to his trailer. He wanted Chelsea to stay with him until she felt ready to be on her own again. He really didn't care how long that took.

As Chelsea drove through the narrow streets of the mobile home park, she could tell that Sweetie was becoming more excited with each dog that she spotted. "You'll have some new friends here," said Chelsea. They drove into the cul-de-sac where her father's mobile home was parked. Immediately, she could see him waving.

Sam had instantly recognized the familiar red, Ford station wagon because it had once belonged to him. Chelsea had needed transportation so he practically gave it to her during one of his visits back up to Meadowview when she was married to Michael. Negative feelings enveloped Sam just as his daughter was pulling into his driveway. His mind coerced his thoughts back to the night his ex-wife had phoned him crying. Darlene told him that Chelsea was going to marry a bum. Whenever he had spoken to Chelsea, Sam had been very careful not to resort to name calling when the subject of Michael came up. But he was certain that Darlene had called Michael a bum and much worse. Sam mentally shook off the unwelcome thoughts and greeted his daughter with a big bear hug.

Her father's hug felt wonderful to Chelsea. Sam scooped the small dog off the ground and they went into his mobile home. Then Sam made his daughter a pitcher of iced tea and added a small amount of mint flavor because it was her favorite beverage. They sipped the tea for a few minutes before they began to bring in Chelsea's belongings. Since it was late in the day, they decided to leave the treadle sewing machine in the car for the time being. Chelsea was pouring both of them another glass of iced tea when the phone started to ring.

Sam looked at his daughter and said, "I'm pretty sure I know who that is." By the tone of his voice Chelsea thought that her father really didn't care to speak to whoever it was. He answered, "Hello. Oh, it's you." Then he placed the telephone receiver on the table and walked away. Since this behavior was so uncharacteristic of her father Chelsea asked, "Who is that?" He replied, "Michael. He's been calling me for several days. He's been drunk each time, but I think he said something about you promising to marry him, but you never showed up for the wedding. Is that true?" Chelsea rolled her eyes and said, "Yes. It's a long story. I'm sorry he's been bothering you." Sam thought about it for awhile then he softly said, "So you left him standing at the alter. After what he did to you, he had it coming." Chelsea couldn't bridle the air that expelled from her when she remembered that James Burke had spoken those exact words.

Chelsea walked over to the phone and picked it up and listened. Michael's speech was slurred and she imagined that his breath smelled of beer. Her tone was even as she said, "Michael. It's me. What do you want?" After a short silence her father heard her say, "No. Don't bother coming here, because I don't want to see you. My mother was right. I should never have married you." Then she immediately laid the phone down. During the next half hour Sam would intermittently pick it up and listen. Finally, he didn't hear Michael's rambling tirade on the other end. Sam made Chelsea laugh when he said, "Someone's going to have a very large, long distance telephone bill."

After Chelsea and Sam ate what they had always called a breakfast/supper of pancakes and sausage, they took Sweetie for a walk. When the three of them came to a small pier, the dog impatiently pulled on her leash until she reached the end. There she looked into the water and became totally engrossed in watching fish repeatedly come to the surface then dive.

Chelsea looked out toward the open water and told her dad that the Gulf of Mexico looked magnificent as her nostrils took in the smell of the salt water. Sam realized the he hadn't felt this happy in years and said, "Chelsea, I'm so glad to have you here. I hope that you'll stay for a long, long time." That night as she crawled into her bed, Chelsea realized that it was good to be home. Before falling asleep she whispered, "Thank you, Lord."

The next morning Sam told Chelsea that he needed to leave for a while so he could take care of a few things. Chelsea thought it would be fun for Sweetie and her to walk around the mobile home park, so she put Sweetie's leash on and they were off. As they strolled, they were cordially greeted by many people and several dogs. Three streets over from her father's place Chelsea spotted an older mobile home sitting back behind two pine trees. When she saw a sign that read FOR RENT in the front window, she was intrigued. She and her dog began to walk the perimeter of the small home. The front yard was shady and she found a small fenced in area for Sweetie in the back yard. Chelsea was definitely interested in this place!

When they returned home, Chelsea's father was on the telephone. From what she could hear, it sounded like he was trying to arrange for a loan. Chelsea wondered why because she thought that his finances were in good shape.

Sweetie was exhausted from the walk. She quickly ran over to her water dish and noisily drank, then ran into Sam's bedroom and laid down on his bed. Although the dog's antics had brought a grin to Sam's face, after his phone conversation ended Sam seemed preoccupied. Chelsea was hesitant to approach the subject of her father's finances but said, "Dad. I couldn't help but overhear your phone call. Do you need some money?"

Sam smiled and said, "I'm trying to buy this mobile home park. It's a good investment! I've been working here for over a year, and I've learned how to run the place." Sam could almost see the wheels turning in Chelsea's head when she said, "Mother's home sold and the lawyer told me before I left Meadowview that the estate will be finalized in about six weeks. Perhaps I should put the inheritance to good use. How long do you have before this opportunity is gone?" Sam thought for a moment then said, "I need to speak with the present owner. I'll go and see her right now. She lives here in the park."

After her dad left, Chelsea decided to make a meatloaf for lunch. She really didn't need to measure any of the ingredients, because she was very familiar with how to prepare the inexpensive yet filling dish. Chelsea mixed the hamburger, diced squares of bread, bits of onion and green pepper, ketchup, mustard, seasonings, and a couple eggs, then formed it into a loaf and placed it in the oven. She glanced out the kitchen window and saw her father approaching. His steps were very spry when he came through the door. His voice sounded celebratory as he said, "Good news! Mrs. Stewart is willing to wait for up to four months. You and I will be partners Chelsea!" Sam began to dance his daughter around the room. Sweetie was still resting on Sam's bed when she heard the commotion. The dog scrambled down the hall and joined in the celebration.

Chelsea said, "I put a meatloaf in the oven Dad. Would you like to have some macaroni and cheese with it?" They agreed on the menu, so Sam began to cut up small pieces of cheese while his daughter put a large pan of water on the stove to boil the macaroni. As they worked together in the kitchen, Sam felt filled with joy. He suddenly realized that it was as if he and his daughter had never been apart and that things seemed just like they had been while she was growing up.

They waited for the water to boil then threw in the macaroni. While the macaroni softened, Chelsea told her father about the cute little mobile home that she had seen during her walk with Sweetie. Sam explained that the mobile home only had one bedroom but it was in good condition for its age. He said, "If everything works out, you'll be able to live there without paying any rent since we'll be co-owners of the park." Chelsea grew even more excited at the prospect of being part of her father's business, and the idea of having her own place again was very appealing. She said, "Dad, I'd like to go over to that trailer after lunch and get inside." He said, "Sure. I'll go with you. I'll take down the FOR RENT sign."

They ate lunch then Sam, Chelsea and Sweetie walked to the trailer. Once inside Chelsea said, "This place is perfect for us Sweetie. I'll get some cleaning supplies this afternoon." Sam thought he should be feeling a little sad because Chelsea was moving out so soon after her arrival, but he was truly happy and thrilled at the thought of helping her get situated in her new place. He said, "The nearest supermarket is easy to find. I'll draw you a map so you can get those cleaning supplies. I've got to do a few things here in the park this afternoon or I'd take you there myself." Then he gave her the keys to her new home. As an afterthought he added, "Until the purchase is finalized, you'll have to pay rent to Mrs. Stewart."

Later in the day Sam returned to the mobile home his daughter had rented. She had already scrubbed down the entire small bathroom and had started to clean the kitchen cupboards when he walked in. "It smells good in here," said a smiling Sam. Chelsea pointed to the floor and said, "Dad, the flooring throughout this place looks practically brand new." Sam explained that the floors were two years old and that he and the previous renter, Bob Bruning, had become good friends. He said, "Bob was in the flooring business. Unfortunately he was forced to retire due to health issues. He's moved in with his son's family over in Almeda."

Chelsea put away the cleaning supplies and they went out the front door. As she locked the door Chelsea said, "When the purchase of this park is completed, maybe I'll have a cement patio and an awning put in out here." Sam thought it was a good idea and suggested that she could also add a barbecue area and picnic table. Chelsea took one last look at the mobile home and gave a silent thank you to God for blessing her with such a nice place to live.

That evening they walked down to the beach. Sam and Chelsea took turns carrying the wiggly dog along the water's edge. They enjoyed the beach and breezes until it got dark, then the three of them started for home. With Chelsea holding onto the dog's leash, they began to walk up the slight incline towards home. Suddenly, out of nowhere a huge white cat ran across their path. Sweetie pulled on her lease so hard that Chelsea lost hold of it. The two humans ran after the cat and Sweetie, but they went out of sight. Sam told Chelsea not to worry and said that he thought the cat belonged to the owner of the park, Jane Stewart.

When they got to the Stewart home, they found Sweetie in the arms of the lady on her front porch. "Are you looking for this cute little dog?" Jane asked. Chelsea replied, "I'm sorry. She got away from me." Sam introduced his daughter and Jane to each other then he said, "You've already met Sweetie." Chelsea spotted the white cat sitting inside the front window of Jane's home and asked if it had been injured. Jane assured her that the cat was just fine. Chelsea asked what the cat's name was and Jane told her that its name was Midnight. Chelsea looked surprised which caused Jane to say, "That name is my late husband's idea of a joke." They all laughed then Chelsea took her dog and turned to leave. Chelsea noticed that her father seemed to briefly linger before he joined her.

After they were home, Sam poured two glasses of ice water and put an ice cube in the dog's water. They both enjoyed watching the dog paw at the water then the telephone rang. During her father's phone conversation, Chelsea didn't notice that his facial expression changed from happy to serious. He got her attention when he said, "Thanks for calling and telling me. Good-by, Andrea." Chelsea knew that the caller could only be her best friend, Andrea Chambers. She wondered why Andrea would call her father. Sam looked glum when he said, "Andrea thought that you would want to know that Henry Newton has died." The air went out of Chelsea. She asked, "What happened?" He said, "Andrea was told that Henry was working with a crew that was tearing down part of a brick wall on one of the old buildings in downtown Meadowview. Somehow it gave way and fell on him. That's all she was able to find out."

Later Chelsea went to bed but couldn't fall asleep. The news of her father-in-law's death was troubling. Henry Newton had always been very kind to her. In fact, before she and Michael were married Henry and Michael's sister's husband, Asa Wilson, helped her move some of the heavy furniture into the apartment above Asa's garage where she and Michael were going to live. Michael had said that he had something important to do that day. Because of what she now knew about her ex-husband, she wondered what he had really done. Then she realized that she really didn't want to know. Chelsea just couldn't lie there anymore so she got out of bed and went to the small front porch where she found her father already sitting on the glider. Sam looked up and said, "You couldn't sleep either I see." She nodded and sat down next to him. He was able to make her smile when he got up and said, "What this calls for is some coffee flavored ice cream."

The dog was begging for a bite of the sweet treat from inside the trailer as the two humans sat and spooned the ice cream into their mouths while the squeaky glider moved back and forth. Sam wondered out loud how Cora Newton must be taking her husband's death when Chelsea said, "I'm not going back to Meadowview for Henry's funeral. I'll wire some flowers from both of us if that's okay with you." Sam said, "Under the circumstances, I think that's the wise thing to do."

Much to the dog's great disappointment, Sam and Chelsea finished all of the ice cream. When they got inside, Sam turned on the television and found an old movie. Chelsea and the dog snuggled on the couch and soon fell asleep. Sam smiled as he covered them with a soft blanket. He looked down at them before he left the room and thought that his daughter's decision to not attend Henry Newton's funeral was for the best. The Newton family had always reminded him of a spider and its web. Chelsea had gotten caught up in a sticky mess and those people had nearly sucked the life out of her. After Sam crawled into his bed, he silently thanked God for safely freeing his daughter from a very bad situation and bringing her back to him.

The next morning Sam and Chelsea were anxious to get an early start on the day. She sat at the kitchen table and made a list of things that she needed to do. First on her list was to call a flower shop so that a floral arrangement would be delivered for Henry Newton's funeral. Next on the list was to move the old treadle sewing machine out of her car and into her new home. Sam knew that Chelsea needed help with that so they did it immediately after a quick breakfast. With that done, Sam left so he could get started on his maintenance duties within the mobile home park.

By noon, Chelsea had cleaned the entire kitchen, dining area and half the living room. She was thinking about getting a bite to eat when her dad showed up with her lunch. The aroma from the food was wonderful and Chelsea's appetite peaked. She said, "Ummmm. It smells so good. What did you bring?" He replied, "It's homemade chicken and noodles from Jane, uh, Mrs. Stewart. I've already eaten, but I have a few more things to do. I'll come back later and help you finish scrubbing down the walls." Chelsea thanked her father then he hurriedly went to his truck. She watched him head towards Jane Stewart's home. After he was out of her sight she giggled and said, "Jane, uh, Mrs. Stewart, indeed!" Chelsea wondered what it would be like to have Jane as her father's girlfriend. Then she wondered why she wondered that.

By the time Sam returned, Chelsea had just finished washing the last window on the inside. She told her dad that all the walls had been washed down including the insides of the closets. "Tomorrow I'll clean all the floors. I'm sure it won't take too long for the living room carpet to dry." she said. Sam said that he wanted to do some tree trimming out in the front yard while she was cleaning the floors. Chelsea said, "That would be nice, Dad. I've also thought about something that you should do for yourself." Sam gave his daughter a puzzled look. "You've been alone for so long. Maybe it's time for you to date. Perhaps you should ask Jane Stewart to go out to dinner or a movie with you." Sam looked down and shuffled his feet then said, "You think so, huh?" Chelsea said, "You will be taking her lunch dishes back, so why don't you ask her out then."

Chelsea arrived back at Sam's trailer first. She showered and was still towel drying her hair when her dad came home. She couldn't resist asking him how it went with Jane. He grinned and said, "Jane said yes. We're going out to dinner and a movie tomorrow evening." Chelsea smiled and said, "Good for you, Daddy!"

The two of them snacked on crackers and cheese then Sam peeled two bananas for them. He felt happy and said, "Thanks for giving me a shove, Chelsea. I guess I needed it." She smiled and said, "You always were shy, Daddy." Then she told him that she wanted to go for a walk on the beach. Sam thought that sounded like fun.

For much of the day Sweetie had spent her time running from window to window playing tag with a larger mixed breed dog that kept circling the trailer while Chelsea cleaned. When the dog's owner tied the dog to a tree across the street, Chelsea placed a lawn chair next to the living room window so that Sweetie could jump up into it and see the other dog. With her dog completely worn out, Chelsea thought it would be okay to leave her at home.

Later while they were walking to the beach, Chelsea told her dad about the dog that Sweetie had played with through the windows. He told her that the larger dog belonged to a friend of his named, Jim Roberts. Sam said that he and Jim were going to take a drive over to Almeda during the coming week and visit with Bob Bruning. Since Chelsea was moving into Bob's former home, he asked her if she would like to come with them. He said, "I'm sure that Bob will be happy to meet the young lady who will be living in his former home." She thought that sounded like fun as long as she could take Sweetie with them. Sam couldn't see any problem with that.

When they reached the beach Chelsea and Sam strolled leisurely. They both realized that the calming sounds of the waves caused them to feel a peace that was almost tangible. Chelsea told her father that she felt safe in this spot and was beginning to think of it as her oasis. Sam had to agree that this particular part of their world was a place where anyone could let go of negative emotions. Neither of them realized that the other was thanking Almighty God for creating their haven.

It was beginning to get dark so they started walking back towards the mobile home park. When they came to Jane Stewart's street Sam said, "I'll be home later. I'm going to check in with Jane." Chelsea smiled and said, "I'll see you in the morning, Daddy."

Early the next morning Chelsea was awakened by the sound of thunder. Her feeling of melancholy grew stronger with each splat of rain she heard hit the roof of her father's mobile home. It reminded her of the first weekend Michael had left her alone. They had only been married for three weeks when he announced that he had to go away for business reasons. That weekend it never stopped raining. When he returned on Sunday evening, he smelled of beer and his clothes looked as if he had slept in them. When he took off his shirt she saw that he had scratches on his shoulders. When she asked him how he got the scratches, he just fell on their bed and began to snore.

The needs of her dog brought Chelsea back to reality. She got dressed then tied Sweetie out in the yard. She went into the kitchen and found her dad preparing some poached eggs and toast. Sam sensed that his daughter had the doldrums. He softly said, "It's going to take time for you to recover from all the upheaval you've experienced." He paused then said, "I've wondered if your mother and I didn't always do what we should have where you were concerned." She replied, "Dad, you and Mother were great parents. The sound of the rain brought back an unpleasant memory involving Michael." Chelsea thought for a moment then said, "Sometimes I wish that I could just wash out my mind and sweep out the last two years of my life. But since that's not possible, I'm going to try to hurl myself into my life here and enjoy every moment of it." Sam smiled widely and said, " I like your attitude! We both need to, as you put it, hurl ourselves into our lives and enjoy them!"

Chelsea sat down next to the window and watched her dog cringe as lightning flashed in the sky. When she brought Sweetie back inside, Sam was waiting with a towel. The little dog squirmed while Sam lovingly patted her dry. Chelsea watched the scene before her and realized that she was surrounded by love. Suddenly her mood changed. She said, "Sweetie and I have a busy day ahead of us. We're going to clean all the floors then measure the windows. And if there's time I'm going to buy some new curtain rods. Dad, could you please draw me a map to the nearest department store?" He said, "We don't have a department store in Delite, but we do have a very nice Five and Dime store. It's affordable and they carry quite a few items. Since it's raining, I'll drive you there myself after lunch."

By eleven thirty, Chelsea had cleaned all the floors and measured the windows in her new home. She and the dog arrived back at her dad's place just before he came in. He was smiling when he said, "I invited Jane to come shopping with us. I hope it's okay with you." Chelsea said, "I'm looking forward to it!" When the telephone rang, Chelsea answered it. Sam heard his daughter say thank you to someone before she hung up. Then she turned to her dad and said, "That was Jane. She invited us to lunch. We're going to have some leftover chicken and noodles." Sam said, "My mouth is already watering!"

After they ate, the three of them cleaned up Jane's kitchen then Sam drove them to the Five and Dime. Once they were inside the store, Sam was definitely the observer. He watched with interest as the two women browsed and compared prices. He had to admire how they managed to spend an hour in the store even though the only items Chelsea bought were the curtain rods. Jane didn't purchase anything. After they were back in the car Jane said, "This is the most fun I've had in quite awhile. I really enjoyed having another woman to shop with. Chelsea, let's do this again real soon." Then she looked at Sam and said, "Oh, Sam! I don't mean that we should leave you out of the shopping fun!" He said, "Ladies, please feel free to leave me out of your, 'shopping fun', any time!" Both women laughed out loud.

During their drive back to the mobile home park, Chelsea could see that her father and Jane were both feeling a little nervous about their upcoming date that evening. After they dropped Jane off at her home Chelsea said, "Dad. She's very nice. Just be yourself tonight and try not to be nervous." Sam grinned and said, "I never thought I'd live to see the day when my daughter would be giving me dating advice."

Chapter 6

James thought it would be best if he spent a few more days away from his home. Alone and dwelling on his wife, Margot's, infidelity caused him to finally realize that her love affair had wounded him much more deeply emotionally than he had been physically wounded in Southeast Asia. When he came to terms with that understanding, he thought that with time and help from a professional counselor their marriage could get back on the right track. He was sincerely determined to give it his best effort.

James was sitting in the backseat of a cab as it pulled in front of his beautiful, yellow, ranch style home in Almeda. He became alarmed when the cab driver had to let him out in the middle of the street because of the police cars that were lined up along the curb and blocking his driveway. James paid the driver then started to go towards the lawn in front of his house. Several policemen were standing in his front yard and he could hear his neighbors whispering as he approached the front door. Then he heard muffled sounds coming from inside the house before a policeman opened the door to let him in. James recognized the officer instantly. Andy Reynolds had played on the same football team as he had when they were in high school together. When James stepped inside, he was surprised to hear his father call out his name. Lyle Burke rushed over to his son and led him into the kitchen. Lyle said, "There's no easy way to tell you this." Lyle paused briefly and said, "It's Margot. She's gone." James was confused. He asked his father, "Gone? Where did she go?"

Andy had followed Lyle and his son into the kitchen. Andy looked straight into James eyes and softly said, "James, it was an accident. We got a call about a woman brandishing a gun. We were told that shots had been fired. We came to this address, 1155 Mariner Drive. We should have been directed to go to 1155 Mariner Road." Andy was having trouble containing his tears as he continued. "My partner thought the hairbrush that Margot was holding was a gun and shot her." He began to cry but somehow managed to get out, "I'm so sorry we couldn't save her."

That night James tried to wrap his mind around the things that had taken place during his chaotic homecoming. At his parent's insistence, James was spending that night in their home in Whitlock. Even though they were in the next room he felt overwhelmed with anxiety and dread of the future. When it finally hit him that he would never have an opportunity to reconcile with Margot, he began to sob. Both his parents heard their son weeping and rushed in to hold their only child.

The days that followed were almost a blur to him. James was astounded by how many friends Margot had when they paid their respects at the funeral home. He had never met most of them. Many worked at the local electric company with her. Margot's funeral caused a torrent of emotions not only for him, but also for her family. Her mother, Lucille Stalder, had been inconsolable. Raymond Stalder was so angry over his younger sister's death that he vowed to take revenge as he wept over her casket. After the funeral, Andy Reynolds told James that there was going to be a formal inquiry into the shooting. Andy and the officer who had shot Margot would be testifying.

After Margot's funeral, James told his parents that he wanted to stay in his own home in Almeda. That night, the stillness surrounding James played with his mind. Within the house that Margot had chosen and decorated, his emotions were confused, heightened and numbed all at the same time. Although his father had hired a cleaning service to scrub down the bathroom where Margot had died, James couldn't bring himself to even look into that room.

James didn't even bother to turn on the lights before he sat down at the kitchen table. He was mentally pouring over all of the other options that he could have taken on the night Margot confessed her unfaithfulness to him. His thoughts were taking him around in circles when he heard a sound at the back door. He opened the door and all he could see were two, large, bright, yellow eyes staring up at him. James instantly thought of Chelsea Swanson's purple stuffed teddy bear with its bright, yellow, glass button eyes. He heard a meow, then a cat walked into the kitchen as if it owned the place. Its black fur was long and fluffy, but its right back paw was white. James asked, "Where did you come from?"

The cat purred and rubbed up against James. Then it walked over to the corner of the kitchen cabinet and carefully left its scent on it. James poured some milk into a saucer while the impatient cat meowed several more times as if to say, "Hurry! I'm ready for that milk right now!" James watched his new friend greedily lick the milk until the saucer was completely dry. Then the cat walked over to the door and sat down while he looked up at the doorknob. When James opened the door, the animal walked out holding its nose and tail high in the air. Once outside the cat began to clean itself in a methodical manner. James observed the organized ritual for a brief time then softly said, "Goodnight Teddy."

James wandered from room to room for more than half the night. Everywhere he went he found things that reminded him of Margot. Her nightgown was still draped over the back of the chair in their bedroom. He thought momentarily of going to bed, but realized that he wouldn't be able to stay there without her. James briefly wondered if he would ever sleep again. His mother had suggested that perhaps he should get a prescription for sleeping pills, but he had nixed that idea. He finally decided to put the alarm clock on the coffee table in the living room and lie down on the couch.

A few hours later, James was surprised by the clanging sound of the alarm clock. He had actually slept and he couldn't remember having had a nightmare. He went into the bedroom and opened the closet. A familiar smell penetrated his nasal passages when he brushed up against one of Margot's dresses. Her scent hung in the air as he searched for a clean shirt to wear. He showered and dressed then he went to the kitchen. When he opened the cupboard door to get the instant coffee, he spotted Margot's raisin bran cereal. He remembered how she refused to eat any other kind of cereal except for that every morning. He felt cloaked in Margot's essence. The weight of her absence seduced him into a state of utter despair. When he understood how difficult it would be for him to live in their home without her, he began to weep. He thought briefly of asking for one more day off from work, but realized that staying at home wouldn't make things any better.

Across town the officer who had accidentally shot Margot Burke wasn't faring much better. Deidra Smith had taken to her bed right after the shooting. Her husband was trying to do everything he could to comfort her, but nothing seemed to work. Bryan Smith felt helpless when his wife refused to eat anything from the tray that he brought to her. He tried to give her a sleeping pill, but she refused to take it. She was just lying in bed staring up at the ceiling.

Deidra sat up in the bed after Bryan left their bedroom. She was overcome with nausea by the smell of the food coming from the tray that he left. And she certainly wasn't about to take any medication. Deidra wanted to have her wits about her. Then she heard Bryan talking on the telephone. She could tell that he was speaking with his boss at the electric company. He was asking for another day off so that he could attend the official inquiry into the shooting with his wife. She heard him say that the hearing was scheduled for ten o'clock in the morning. Feeling terrified, she hoped that the next morning would never come. Deidra knew that she didn't mean to kill Margot Burke. But she also knew that it would surely be her doomsday if the truth that Margot had at one time been Bryan's lover ever got out.

Deidra recollected the times when she followed Bryan to his trysts. It had been easy to spy on him and his lover. They never even suspected. She could have predicted that Bryan would take Margot Burke to the Dew Drop Inn because that's where she and Bryan had met when Deidra was married to Vince Chelsea. Sourly she spoke aloud, "You didn't even try to change your routine, Bryan." He appeared instantly after he heard the sound of her voice. He asked, "Do you need anything?" Deidra didn't even want to look at him. She just laid her head back down on the pillow and stared up at the ceiling and began to lose herself within a small crack in the plaster up there. Then she shivered at the thought of going to prison for murder. Her husband saw the shiver and gently covered her with a blanket.

The next morning James and his parents arrived early at the county courthouse. They were surprised to find Margot's family already standing just inside the double-doored entrance. A man came over to the group and led them down a large hall and into an opulent room with an ornate wooden desk. They had been seated there for about five minutes when Andy Reynolds, a female police officer and several men in suits entered through a side door. As the group passed by, Margot's brother, Raymond Stalder, gave the female officer an angry glare. An uneasy silence permeated the room until Judge Kenneth Pearce came in and sat down behind the large wooden desk. The judge said something, but unfortunately James missed it because his mind had wandered. He'd been thinking of a red, Ford station wagon, a beautiful dark-haired woman, and a bug-eyed Boston Terrier. James shook his head and felt guilty for thinking about Chelsea Swanson.

James senses pulled him back to the present when he watched Andy Reynolds swear an oath to tell the truth. After stating his name and spelling it, Andy said that after he and his partner arrived at 1155 Mariner Drive, he wasn't able to see into the front of the house. He said he'd gone around to the back of the home and had just entered the kitchen through an outside door from the patio. That's when he heard the sound of a single gunshot. He immediately ran to where it came from and found Officer Smith standing in the hallway and holding her gun just outside of the bathroom. That was all that he had witnessed.

After Andy returned to where he had been seated, Deidra Smith was called to testify. She appeared a bit unsteady when she got out of her chair. Deidra stood before the court and also swore an oath to tell the truth, then sat down. An attorney was about to ask his first question, but before he could get out a word, Deidra Smith fainted. She fell off the chair and onto the floor. Everyone could see a bloody gash on her left temple. When she came to, she wasn't able to sit up. Almost everyone there was moved by the sight of her husband kneeling over her and gently caressing her face. After several minutes it was obvious that the woman wouldn't be able to continue. As her husband was carrying her out of the room Raymond Stalder angrily muttered, "What a masterful performance that was."

Judge Pearce gave Raymond a stern look then stated that he would allow the hearing to continue without the testimony of Officer Smith. James couldn't understand how the inquiry could go forward without the main witness, but remained silent.

Margot's brother, Raymond, on the other hand couldn't accept the ruling and he said so. He erupted with some very loud comments about the continuance being part of a cover up. Then Raymond became even more belligerent when the judge said, "Please exercise some decorum Mr. Stalder. Another outburst will not be tolerated." That was all it took to make Raymond livid. He jumped up and his chair tipped over. A scuffle ensued and in the end Raymond was physically escorted out of the room by two burly guards.

After the ruckus, the judge asked the mayor of Almeda to make a brief statement. He said, "Mrs. Burke's untimely death was the result of an accidental shooting. We are presently implementing procedures and street name changes so that this sort of thing will never happen again." Then he personally apologized to James and the Stalder family. With that, the formal inquiry ended. Caught off guard, James suddenly found himself shaking hands with several men wearing suits while a photographer snapped a few pictures. That made James feel very uncomfortable, so he got out of there just as fast as he could.

The photographer followed the stunned group out to the sidewalk in front of the courthouse and began to take more pictures. A reporter tried to interview James, but he kept walking toward his father's vehicle. Lyle Burke struggled with wanting to protect his son from the prying reporter or go over and extend his sympathy to the Stalder family. He watched his wife go to Margot's mother and embrace her. Catherine Burke and Lucille Stalder had tears running down their cheeks. Although the sad scene was heart wrenching, it was just too captivating for the photographer to pass up. Raymond Stalder approached the photographer immediately after he snapped the picture. Margot's brother wanted to grab the camera out of Delmer Davis' hands and smash it. But with the two burly guards still standing close by, he went to his mother and gently put his arm over her shoulders and led her to their car.

The two men from the newspaper silently watched as the Stalder and Burke cars pulled away. Delmer Davis looked down at his camera and felt a little guilty. He had intentionally intruded upon what should have been a private moment just because he wanted the Stalder and Burke families' tragic story to be the main feature on his newspaper's front page.

By the time James and his parents arrived at his home in Almeda, Lyle and Catherine realized that their son was mentally and physically used up. They decided to stay with him for the rest of the day. Although Lyle seldom thought that it was a good idea for Catherine to pamper their son, he wasn't going to stand in her way this time. He watched as she hovered over James as only a mother can. She was determined to get her son to take in some nourishment. Somehow she managed to get him to eat a bowl of chicken noodle soup for lunch.

Later in the afternoon Catherine told her husband that she thought they should stay with James that night. He had to agree. The three of them spent the rest of the day playing card games at the kitchen table just as they had done when James was growing up. Lyle said that he wanted to make his special, homemade egg salad sandwiches with small pieces of celery in it for dinner. They all thought that sounded good. James decided to make a pitcher of mint flavored iced tea just because it was his mother's favorite beverage. Catherine enjoyed watching her two guys prepare the evening meal.

When they were finished eating, Catherine said that she would do the dishes because her men had prepared supper. She had just finished cleaning up when she heard a sound at the kitchen door. She was curious so she opened it. A fluffy, long-haired black cat walked in, then went over and sat down in front of the refrigerator. Catherine and Lyle were surprised when James said, "Teddy. You're back!" His mother asked James, "When did you get a cat?" He replied, "Oh, he's not mine. He just showed up." Lyle asked, "How do you know his name?" James thought about Chelsea Swanson and her stuffed bear as he said, "His eyes remind me of a teddy bear I once saw." Catherine said, "He's black with just one white foot. You should call him White Foot." Lyle said, "Teddy is his first name. His last name should be Whitefoot." James said, "His full name is now Teddy Whitefoot."

James poured a small amount of milk into a saucer and placed it on the floor. Teddy quickly devoured the milk. When the cat was finished, Lyle picked him up. He noticed that the cat was wearing a collar. With that observation he said, "This cat must have an owner."

Teddy purred while Lyle petted him. However, the cat soon let Lyle know that it was time to put him down when it tried to wriggle out of his arms. Lyle put him on the floor and Teddy walked over to the back door. Catherine opened it and he marched out with his nose and tail held high in the air just as he had done before. The three humans watched the cat sit down on the cement patio and perform the feline cleaning ritual. Teddy licked his front paws and used them to wipe his face and ears. Then, he very noisily lapped his tongue over his entire body. They all admired the precise movements of the animal and hoped to encounter him again in the future.

The next morning on the other side of the town of Almeda, Deidra Smith was alone in her home. Bryan had decided that it was time for him to get back to his job with the electric company. Deidra actually welcomed the solitude. She cracked the bedroom window to get a breath of fresh air and saw a robin land in her front yard. It flew up and out of her sight and she was wishing that she could fly away with it when Bryan's truck pulled into the driveway. She looked at the alarm clock and saw that it was a few minutes after twelve o'clock noon. Deidra desperately hoped that her husband wasn't going to try to get her to eat lunch with him. She was still feeling sick to her stomach.

When he came into their bedroom the concern on Bryan's face was very evident. He said, "Deidra, I brought you some orange juice. If you're not going to eat, at least you should drink this juice." She thanked him and took a sip because she could see that he was sincerely trying to take care of her.

It wasn't long before Bryan left for work again and Deidra dozed off. She was soon awakened because of the grizzly nightmare that she had of the shooting. She sat on the edge of the bed and held her head in her hands. She wondered how she could ever live with herself after what she had done.

Deidra got out of bed and went into the living room. She turned on the television because she preferred listening to the meaningless noise it would emit to reliving over and over again the sound of the gunshot that her mind couldn't silence. Fervently, she wanted to escape the constant replaying of the day when Margot Burke died. But instead, she recalled that day was the first day of her part-time job with the Almeda Police Department.

When they got the radio call Deidra felt anxious, but Andy Reynolds assured her that everything would be just fine. After they got to the Burke home, Andy couldn't see in the front window because the drapes were drawn closed. Then he had decided to go around to the back of the home.

Deidra had been left standing in front of the open, two-car garage. There was an older, cream-colored Pontiac sedan parked on the right side and on the left there was a newer, green Dodge pickup truck. She decided to go into the garage. Once inside, Deidra scanned the garage and spotted the side door to the house. As she walked over to it, she wondered if the door would open. When she carefully turned the knob, it did. She peered through the crack and saw a refrigerator. She pushed the door open a little farther and stepped in. While standing in the kitchen, Deidra could hear sounds but she couldn't tell from where they were coming. Although she felt very afraid, she walked through the kitchen and went into the living room. Her eyes hadn't yet adjusted to the diminished light as she moved into a darkened hallway and listened. Deidra instinctively took out her sidearm when she heard another sound. Walking a little ways down the hall she caught sight of someone in a side room. The person was a woman and when she lifted her hand it looked like she was pointing a gun straight at Deidra. In a split second Deidra fired her weapon at the other woman in self-defense. Andy appeared immediately after that. Later that morning Deidra was told that the woman had in fact been holding a black hairbrush and that her name was Margot Burke.

That afternoon in another part of the town of Almeda, Bryan Smith wasn't able to concentrate. His tormented heart desired for his thoughts to be only of his sweet wife, but the memory of Margot Burke sabotaged his mind. He had fallen deeply in love with Margot and had wanted to get a divorce so he could marry her. But Margot had ended their relationship when her husband was wounded in Southeast Asia. Bryan had pleaded with Margot to stay with him even though she kept telling him that she could never love anyone except James Burke.

When Bryan learned of her death, he honestly wanted to die himself. During Margot's funeral his emotions became uncontrollable. Before the service ended he had to make a quick exit. When he went back to his car he wanted to get away fast, but was so blinded with tears he almost pulled out into the path of another car. The next day at work, one of his coworkers asked him why he left before Margot's service was over. He had said it was because he was feeling ill, which wasn't a total lie. Even though it was Deidra who shot Margot, on some level Bryan felt responsible for her death.

That same afternoon, Sam Swanson, his daughter Chelsea and Jim Roberts went to the home on Mariner Drive in Almeda where Bob Bruning lived with his son. It was a beautiful, white ranch style home with an immaculately kept lawn. Unbeknownst to Chelsea, it sat right next to James Burke's home. As Chelsea walked up the Bruning's driveway, her eyes were drawn to the lovely yellow, ranch style home on her left. Suddenly, an unexplained awareness that she couldn't understand poured over Chelsea, but she shook it off.

Chelsea decided to pick Sweetie up while keeping the leash attached just before the group entered through the Bruning's front door. Once inside, Sam made the introductions and Mr. Bruning was very happy to meet the young woman and her dog who had moved into his previous home. However, it was soon very obvious that his son's wife was not exactly thrilled. The woman gave the dog a disapproving look and Chelsea was glad that Sweetie was held safely within her arms. After a few minutes Chelsea excused herself and went back outside. She put Sweetie down and they walked down the driveway until they reached the street. Then Chelsea made a vow to herself and the dog that in the future she would bear in mind how others might react to Sweetie's presence.

Sweetie tugged on her leash and pulled Chelsea out into the street. Chelsea looked all around the neighborhood. She could tell that the homes on this street were expensive. When she took a second look at the yellow house next to the Bruning home, she decided that it was her favorite but didn't know why. Suddenly, the dog snorted with excitement. Chelsea looked in the same direction as the dog. Sweetie was intently watching a fluffy black cat that was sitting directly under a tree in the front yard of the yellow home grooming itself. Soon Chelsea realized that her grip on the dog's leash was not as strong as the dog's determination to run over to the cat. Sweetie was on that poor cat before it knew what had happened. Chelsea watched as the cat seemed to jump a good eight feet high in the air. In an instant the cat twisted around just in time to grab onto a branch of the tree. By the time Chelsea got there, the dog was circling under the tree and whimpering like a puppy. The only way Chelsea could catch her dog was by stepping on its leash.

Sweetie struggled in Chelsea's arms after being gathered up and taken back over to the car. The doggy wasn't at all happy with her situation when Chelsea put her in and shut the door. Soon her father and Jim Roberts returned. An obviously upset Chelsea pointed to the adjacent yard and told them that she needed to check on a cat that her dog had chased up a tree.

When she got there Chelsea looked up to the branch where the cat had been, but couldn't see it. She wondered if it climbed down and ran away. Finally the cat meowed and she spotted it but only because of its white, right back paw. Chelsea walked around the tree and tried repeatedly to coax the cat down, but it just wouldn't budge. She walked to the front door and knocked several times, but no one answered. Chelsea was extremely disappointed and felt the same awareness that she had experienced earlier. When she realized that there was nothing else she could do, she went back to the car. As they were driving away, Jim Roberts told

Chelsea not to be worried and said, "I'm sure you've heard it said that cats have nine lives."

The car in which Chelsea Swanson was riding had just driven out of sight when James Burke pulled into his driveway. When he got out of his truck, he immediately heard Teddy's distressed meows. He walked to the tree and looked up. James soon discovered that the cat seemed to be stranded on one of the top branches. He thought it odd the cat had climbed up so high. When James tried to talk Teddy Whitefoot down out of the tree, he wouldn't cooperate. Out of desperation James went to his garage and brought back a ladder. He leaned it against the tree and climbed up. After a few seconds the cat carefully crawled across the branch it was on and James was able to get hold of him. Once Teddy was rescued, he merely walked away without even looking back. James had to grin as he said, "Ingrate."

James returned the ladder to its hanging place in the garage and was about to go into the house. When he heard an engine of a vehicle in his driveway, he turned to see Raymond Stalder's car. James walked out of the garage and down the driveway to greet his brother-in-law. Before James even got to the car he could tell by the look on Raymond's face that he was fuming. The angry man jumped out and charged toward James shaking the newspaper he was holding. "How could you let them get away with this? They're covering their backsides!" roared Raymond. On the front page of the local paper were some pictures of James shaking hands with several of the town's political leaders.

James wasn't willing to deal with this situation while standing out in his driveway because that snooty, nosy neighbor, Renee Bruning, was watching them from a window. As she scrutinized the two men, James tried to appear as though he wasn't gesturing in her direction when he said, "Let's go inside where we'll be able to discuss this in private." Raymond remembered that Margot had referred to Renee Bruning as a busybody, so he took the hint and followed James through the garage and into the house.

The men sat down at the kitchen table and were silent for a while. James spoke first. Shaking his head he said, "I shouldn't have left. If I had stayed, maybe things wouldn't have turned out this way." Raymond looked at James and said, "Margot told Mother that she said something that caused you to become upset and leave. I'd like to know what she said to you."

Raymond could hear the tears in James voice as he said, "She said that she didn't want there to be any secrets between us and told me that she had an affair when I was overseas. She said that it ended when she found out that I was wounded. I went away to think. After I did that, I knew I needed to come back and work things out with her because I love her!"

Neither of them could keep from crying. They just sat there silently weeping without speaking. Raymond was feeling so confused. He was not only struggling with the loss of Margot, but now he had to deal with finding out that his sister had been unfaithful to her husband. The man felt emotionally barren, but managed to stand and slowly walk toward the door to the garage. James followed him. They walked out of the garage and stood briefly at the top of the driveway. There the look on Raymond's face depicted his feeling of hopelessness. He said, "Something just doesn't feel right about my little sister's death." James felt his throat tighten because he thought Raymond looked almost lifeless before he watched him walk down the driveway. Then Raymond got into his car and gave James a halfhearted wave before backing out and driving away.

James watched his brother-in-law drive down the road and out of his sight. Then he wondered if the whole truth would ever become known to anyone who loved Margot. When he felt eyes on him, he realized that Renee Bruning was looking at him. He nodded to the woman and stepped back inside the garage and pulled the door down from the inside.

He returned to the kitchen and was feeling very tired so he decided to take a shower. James went to the bedroom and began to undress. After he took off his shirt and pants, he looked toward the bed and images of Margot immediately filled his thoughts. Suddenly the sickening memory of the night she confessed her love affair with another man confronted him. He had been sitting on the side of the bed and had just taken off his prosthetic leg. Right after she told him about her affair, he became enraged and threw the leg clear across the room. It had landed in the upholstered chair. That's when Margot blurted out that she wanted him to tell her that he forgave her because she needed to hear him say it. When she made that demand, he became even angrier. She watched him hop over to the closet and pull out his crutch. She didn't say anything when he took off his wedding band and put it in her hand. He remembered how he had lingered for a moment, but Margot had remained silent. That had caused his lividity to grow massive.

James senses came back to the present when he felt his entire body begin to shake. He sat down on the bed so he could remove the plastic leg. Once it was off he held it in his trembling hands and stared at the appendage without really seeing it for a long while. He was surprised when the face of Chelsea Swanson appeared in his mind. Imagining that she probably wondered why he used a crutch instead of a prosthetic leg caused him to want to touch her. Later while showering, James felt ashamed for thinking of Chelsea Swanson just as he had during the legal hearing that inquired into Margot's accidental shooting. He sincerely wanted to detach himself from his own emotions, but instead his tears began to mingle with the water that was falling from the showerhead.

That evening Chelsea's mind was on the black cat with one white, back paw and the conversation that had taken place between Jim Roberts and her father during their drive back from Almeda to the mobile home park in Delite. She was still concerned for the cat and hoped it was okay. Chelsea shook her head and thought it was so sad that the woman who lived in the lovely yellow house next to the Bruning home had been accidentally shot to death. Jim and her father had said that the Bruning's neighbor had died when the Almeda police had mistaken the black hairbrush she was holding for a gun. The woman's husband hadn't been home that morning, and by the time he arrived that afternoon it was too late. After Chelsea went to bed, she asked God to please provide comfort to the family of the woman who had died.

The next morning James rubbed the sleep out of his eyes and was grateful that his troubled dreams hadn't been extremely disturbing. He did remember that he had awakened briefly a couple times, but he'd been able to immediately fall back to sleep. He went into the kitchen and put the kettle on the stove. While reaching for the instant coffee, he looked out the window and saw Teddy Whitefoot walking toward the shed in his backyard. He decided that he would try to find the cat's owner that night after he got home from work.

James spooned the coffee into the cup and waited for the kettle to whistle. He picked up the newspaper that Raymond had left on the kitchen table the previous evening. He studied the pictures of himself shaking hands with the politicians and mischievously chuckled out loud as he wondered if anyone who shook his hand that day might have caught his creepin' crud. James' mood soon turned to one of gloom, however, when he remembered how Margot would rush around the kitchen completely dressed except for her bare feet before she left for work each morning. He wasn't able to prevent his mind from bringing forth the sounds of her bare feet tapping on the kitchen floor so sadness overpowered him.

Chapter 7

Chelsea had fallen into a daily routine during the seven months since she had made the transition from Meadowview, New York to Delite, Florida. She found a job working part-time as a teller in a local bank and the money she made from that job had been just enough to pay for the essentials. Even though her savings had been meager when she came to Florida, she had dipped into it only once. She caressed her new bed's early American headboard with its rich, dark wood and thought that it was worth every penny she'd paid for it. Not that she wasn't grateful to her father for loaning her the use of his folding, rollaway bed with the metal bar right in the middle of it. No matter where she had tried to lay on it, that bar had dug itself deep into her back. But at last after only three nights in the new bed, her backache was gone!

She was very thankful for the money that she had inherited from the sale of her mother's small, cottage home. Chelsea hadn't doubted for one second about her dad's business savvy. It was right on the mark. He had told her that the mobile home park would be a good investment and it was. As a result of her partnership in her father's business, Chelsea's monthly finances weren't as tight as they had been. But what was even more important to Chelsea was how she was feeling about herself. She no longer felt like she was imprisoned in loveless surroundings and hopeless circumstances. Instead her life was filled with happy days either working at the bank or performing maintenance chores here in the park.

She walked down the hallway and into the living room. Chelsea couldn't believe her good fortune and said a prayer of thanks when she looked at the used furniture that Jane Stewart had given to her. Jane's garage and storage building were chocked-full of items that people had left when they moved away from the mobile home park.

Jane had explained that when she was a child during the great depression, her family had to move many times so that her father could get some work. She said her parents had always managed to take their possessions with them, but she told Chelsea about some neighbors who had lost everything because they mortgaged all that they owned to purchase a farm. Then they went bust. The man, his wife and their three children left their home with only the clothes on their backs and what they could carry. Witnessing the misfortune of that family had caused Jane to become very thrifty and to also save anything that was usable whenever a tenant of the mobile home park left something behind. Some of the stuff had been sitting in the buildings for many years.

Chelsea didn't have time to daydream this morning. Earlier in the week Jane had invited Sam and Chelsea to come with her to the small church in Delite that she attended. Without dawdling, Chelsea grabbed a quick bite to eat and got ready. She hadn't gone to church for far too long and was really looking forward to it.

Before leaving Chelsea wanted to play Sweetie's latest game. Every morning since Chelsea had gotten her new bed, the little dog had jumped into the middle of the covers when Chelsea tried to pull them up. The dog anxiously waited outside the bathroom for her human to finish dressing, then ran toward the bedroom. When Chelsea started to make the bed, the playful tug-of-war began. Sweetie plopped down right in the middle of the bed so that Chelsea could only smooth out the sheets and bedspread around her. After the bed was made, it looked perfect to Chelsea because Sweetie was curled up in its center.

Later that morning, Chelsea received the spiritual food that she truly required from the minister's sermon. She had long needed to become strong enough to let go of her troubled past. When she surrendered her mind, body and soul to God, she suddenly realized that she had been foolishly punishing herself by withholding the only true nourishment she required which were His words. Chelsea felt spiritually reborn because at last she could understand that God had carried her through all the bad experiences, including her prideful partnership with self-pity. Silently she thanked God for granting His peace to her.

Before closing the service, the minister announced that on the following Thursday evening at 7:00 o'clock the first Young Adult's Group meeting and covered dish would be held in the church's event hall. Jane and Sam encouraged Chelsea to place her name on the sign up sheet at the table in the back of the church. The pastor's wife asked her to bring a cake and salad. Although Chelsea wasn't quite sure if she wanted to become a member of the group, she committed to the first meeting.

During the week that followed Chelsea was very busy. Thursday night seemed as though it came upon her before she was prepared. She had already tossed the garden salad and the chocolate cake was cooled. Jane had given her an easy, no fail, creamy chocolate icing recipe and it went on smoothly and quickly. With the food prepared and placed in their containers, Chelsea showered and washed her hair. Earlier in the week she'd had her waist length hair cut to a more manageable shoulder length. She realized that it wouldn't be dry by the time she reached the church, but there just wasn't enough time to wait for that to happen.

Lately Chelsea felt that she had been running behind schedule more often than not, especially today. What with helping her father with some dusty chores in the mobile home park during the day and trying to prepare the food for tonight's church group meeting, she was rushing like the wind in order to leave on time. She got outside and had just locked her front door when her father and Jane came walking up.

"Jane and I have something to show you," said Sam. Jane shyly held out her left hand. She was wearing a beautiful diamond ring. Chelsea sat the cake and salad down on the picnic table. As she hugged Jane and then her father, tears of pure joy came into her eyes. Chelsea said, "I'm so happy for all of us! You two belong together. I'm glad that you found each other."

After their embrace Sam kissed his daughter on her forehead. Then he picked up the salad and cake and said, "You'll be late if you don't leave right now." After he placed the food on the front seat of her car, the group shared a three-way hug.

When she arrived, the parking lot at the church had about two-dozen cars in it. Chelsea thought she was too late and felt a little embarrassed because her hair was still damp. But she decided to press ahead and go into the church's event hall. She struggled with holding onto the food as she tried to open the side door. Chelsea felt the knob turn from the other side as the door began to open. The minister's wife, Haley Applegate, told Chelsea that she would hold the door open so that the food wouldn't get spilled. It seemed to Chelsea that Haley was one of those people who are always truly and perpetually happy. Chelsea's perception of Haley's constant joy was contagious. It caused Chelsea to feel instantly at ease as they walked through the door.

The hum of various conversations became louder as the two women entered the large room. Chelsea didn't notice the red-haired young man that turned to watch her. He had seen her in church during the last worship service and hoped that she would come for this first meeting of the Young Adult's Group.

Chelsea realized that she wasn't late when the minister asked everyone to form a circle and hold hands. After Chelsea put the salad and cake on the food table, she joined Haley and her husband in the circle. Rev. Adam Applegate began the meeting with a prayer then laughingly said, "After a very short meeting because I haven't eaten anything since this morning, we'll dig into all of this good smelling food." Then he held up a paper with lines on it that contained most of the signatures of the folks who were there and said, "And if anyone hasn't signed this yet, please do so."

The meeting was indeed held in haste when a very attractive young man with red hair and an engaging smile said, "The purpose of the Young Adult's Group is essentially to find worthy work projects in order to perform tasks that will improve our community. Now let's eat!"

After the circle of people broke up Chelsea decided to retreat to a quiet corner. She waited to see how many people were going to the food line. Everyone seemed to be headed for the food so she went to sign the paper. When it was her turn, she wrote her name within the space allotted then went to the food line.

Haley Applegate looked through the crowd of people and spotted her twin brother. She felt a deep concern for him because he had recently separated from his wife, Deidra. He looked up and smiled at her. Haley felt a little less stressed when he did that. She walked over to where he was standing and said, "Bryan, I believe yours' is the last signature we need before we can start

cutting out the names and placing the strips of paper in a bucket."
Bryan Smith quickly signed his name under Chelsea Swanson's
then followed her to the food line. Haley watched her brother
walk away and was feeling grateful to God for answering her
many prayers. Just that morning Bryan told her that he had
stopped drinking and would no longer be frequenting bars.

Bryan Smith stood behind Chelsea Swanson and saw up
close that she had cut her beautiful hair. He also noticed that it
was still damp from being washed. Chelsea was completely
oblivious of her admirer. Bryan watched her fill her plate, get an
iced tea then look around until she found an empty table. She was
still unaware of the red-haired man shadowing her, but his sister
saw everything. Haley got to them just before Bryan sat down
next to Chelsea. Haley said, "Chelsea, I'd like for you to meet my
twin brother, Bryan Smith." The resemblance was easy to see.
They both had honey-red hair and light brown eyes. Their smiles
revealed straight white teeth and Chelsea was immediately
fascinated with Haley's twin. She said, "I'm happy to meet you,
Bryan."

Haley excused herself, but before she turned to leave she
heard her brother ask, "Why did you cut off your long hair?"
Haley saw the surprised look on Chelsea's face and was about to
chastise her brother for being impolite. Then Haley saw her new
friend smile sweetly as she said, "I'm hoping that having shorter
hair will be less of a hassle for me." Haley walked away from the
two of them smiling. She had no way of knowing that Chelsea
Swanson would have undoubtedly gobbled down some food and
made a quick exit if Bryan Smith hadn't sat down next to her. In
fact, Chelsea was beginning to think that tonight was going to be
a really fun evening after all.

When they had all finished eating, Pastor Applegate
explained that there would be an activity that would require
everyone to have a partner. Haley stirred the papers in the bucket
that contained everyone's name with a large wooden spoon. Then
her husband began to draw them out one by one. Bryan and
Chelsea were surprised when their names were partnered with
each other, but Haley wasn't. Rev. Adam Applegate realized that
his lovely wife was playing cupid but he didn't see any harm in it.

After everyone had a partner Adam said, "Each one of us must find out one important fact about our partner." Chelsea wondered what type of important fact the pastor had in mind. But when Bryan volunteered that he worked for the local electric company, Chelsea told him that she did maintenance work in the mobile home park where she lived and that she also worked as a bank teller. As each person revealed what important fact they had learned about their partner, it became clear that everyone had focused on their work or jobs. Rev. Applegate said, "Each of us defines ourselves by what work we do. Since this group has been formed under the conception of working for the betterment of this community, let's all go out into our lives with an awareness of what could be improved where we live, work and play."

Later that evening Chelsea turned into her driveway feeling an emotion that could only be described as joy. She sincerely believed that all aspects of her life could not be better. Although she hadn't heard bells, Chelsea was fully aware of and flattered by Bryan Smith's attention. But she couldn't help but feel nervous because of what had happened when she rushed into a marriage with Michael. The trepidation was so strong, that Chelsea decided not to be too hasty with making a permanent commitment.

When she reached her front door it opened. Chelsea wondered why her father was there and why he looked so distressed. She immediately asked, "What's wrong Dad?" He replied, "This was delivered to my mailbox." Chelsea studied the envelope and noticed that it was from Michael and that the return address was the Great Lakes Naval Training Center. Sam said, "Michael must have joined the Navy."

Chelsea put the letter in her purse and told her dad that she would read it later because she didn't want her good mood to be spoiled. Then she told her father all about her evening with the Young Adult's Group including meeting the twin brother of the young pastor's wife. Chelsea thought she should reassure her father so she said, "I won't let Michael hurt me ever again, Daddy."

Chelsea had deliberately put off reading Michael's letter until the weekend. When she awoke early, her curiosity lured her to her purse. She didn't realize that her hands were trembling as she removed the envelope and slowly opened it. Her heart skipped a beat when she was faced with Michael's familiar script. She remembered the times before they were married when he came into the bank when she was working just to personally pass a handwritten love note through her teller's window. Then he would wink at her and quietly leave. She was fighting back tears as she read.

Dear Chelsea,

I'm doing better than I have in years. I hope that you are too. I've stopped drinking and have joined the U. S. Navy. I'm a much better person for it.

After my dad died I began to understand why I drank so much. I used liquor to dull my senses instead of facing the truth about my life. My mother had always prevented me from having a relationship with Dad. She even used me to get back at him.

On the day of Dad's funeral I went to the funeral home early because I wanted to be alone with him one last time. That's when I found a woman weeping over him. She didn't know who I was and told me that Dad and she had been in love for many years. In fact, they had two sons together. Mother and my sister, Linda, knew about it but they never told me. Then later in the lawyer's office we were told that Dad left half of his estate to his other family. Mother said that I had to help her fight the other family in court. That's when I knew I had to make some changes. I sobered up and got out of Meadowview.

I can honestly say that you are the best person that I've ever had in my life! And I deeply regret everything that I said and did that hurt you! I know I don't deserve it, but I'm asking for your forgiveness. I would be privileged and honored to have you back in my life again. I will understand if you are not interested in pursuing my offer. Please reply either way.

Love,
Michael

Chelsea reread the letter several more times. It took some time for her to digest Michael's words. She didn't want to be alone with her thoughts so she grabbed the dog and they walked to her father's trailer. Before she could knock he opened the door.

Sam had been frying some bacon when he noticed movement outside his kitchen window. He had pushed the frying pan off the burner and watched his daughter's determined stride as she approached his trailer. As she had gotten closer he could see the intense look on her face. When she stepped into his trailer she handed him Michael's letter and asked him to please read it. Sam instantly felt a flash of anger toward the man who had hurt his little girl, but that emotion soon faded as he began to read. After careful consideration Sam softly said, "It certainly sounds as though Michael is a changed man. I don't know how to advise you." He paused to study her sweet face, but couldn't tell what she was thinking. Finally Sam said, "Maybe you don't really need my advice."

Chelsea sat down on his couch and unleashed Sweetie. She wasn't sure what she should be feeling as she picked up the dog and hugged her. Having been very well acquainted with the feelings of confusion and sadness while he was married to Chelsea's mother, Darlene, Sam could easily recognize and understand those emotions in his daughter's demeanor. After a brief moment Chelsea said, "I just wanted to share the letter with you, Dad. That's all."

The knock on the front door hardly distracted Sweetie from her quest to gain a bite or two of the aromatic bacon. The dog was standing on her hind legs and begging when Jane came in carrying a carton of eggs. Sam explained that he had forgotten to buy any. Chelsea thought that she was interrupting a romantic breakfast and was about to excuse herself when Jane said that she was happy to see her and asked Chelsea to join them. The invitation couldn't have come at a better time as far as Chelsea was concerned. She was more than happy to stay and told Jane and her father that the food, and especially the company, were a most welcome distraction for her.

After breakfast, Chelsea offered to clean up the kitchen, but Sam and Jane said that it wasn't necessary. Chelsea was tickled when the two of them began giving each other flirtatious looks as they gathered the dishes from the table. Considering what she was observing, Chelsea told them that she would be driving herself to church that morning. While walking home, Chelsea was amazed and delighted because her mood had so quickly gone from being a dismal feeling of confusion to lightheartedness. She thanked God for His presence and for Jane and her father.

During her drive to church Chelsea felt somewhat ashamed because this was only the second time she had attended a worship service since she had left Meadowview. She remembered how her mother had gone to church faithfully every week. Chelsea thought of herself as a backslider and was thankful that God had provided her with a good role model when it came to church attendance. Even though Chelsea often felt confused by her mother's seemingly tormented life, habitual church attendance was something that always seemed to come easy for Darlene Langston Swanson.

As she drove, Chelsea's mind took her back to the summer when her parents told her the truth about her biological father. At first she had been in shock. The idea of having been fathered by a man she had never known seemed so unreal to her. Then the day came when her dad moved to Florida. The weeks that followed had been a very difficult period of time.

Chelsea's thoughts were brought back to the present when she had to brake for a stop sign. When there was a lull in the traffic, she pulled onto the main highway. She drove under the overpass to Whitlock and her mind again wandered. Chelsea remembered how she had struggled with coming to terms with knowing that there was blood coursing through her veins from an unknown man. It had been her very best friend, Andrea Chambers, who had encouraged her to search for him.

The two girls had borrowed a car from one of Andrea's brothers. The old wreck didn't look like much, but it got them safely to Buffalo, New York on a Saturday morning. They pulled into a service station for some gas. Then they had spotted a phone booth. While Andrea took care of getting the car gassed up,

Chelsea walked over to take a look at the telephone book. She recalled that her father had told her about a man named Peterson who owned a dry-cleaning establishment. She found that name in the yellow pages and wrote down the address. They thanked the attendant and asked for directions to Peterson's Dry Cleaners. Then Andrea had driven her nervous friend to the business.

When they got there Chelsea almost backed out due to fear, and yet felt compelled by her desire to know the truth. Andrea had held her hand for moral support as they walked into the old brick building. Chelsea remembered how she had difficulty introducing herself to the clerk because she was so anxious. But then she'd somehow managed to ask if it would be possible to meet the owner, Mr. Peterson. Shortly after that an elderly gentleman came to the counter. Her voice had trembled when she said, "Hello. I'm Chelsea Swanson. Perhaps you may remember my mother's father. His name was Theo Langston."

Mr. Peterson had immediately invited her into his office. Chelsea looked to Andrea for encouragement, and then followed the man. When they entered the small room, he motioned to a chair and she sat down. Then he gestured to all of the framed photographs on the office walls and said, "These folks are my family. That picture beside you was taken of my daughter, Ellen, on her wedding day." Chelsea turned to look at a black and white photo of a lovely young woman who was standing next to a very handsome, dark-haired man. Without thinking Chelsea had blurted out, "Is that man my father?" She had been embarrassed by the all too sudden question and wondered if Mr. Peterson would ask her to leave. But instead, Simon Peterson had smiled kindly and said, "You look like Tony De Salvo, and you probably are his daughter."

It had taken a few moments for Chelsea to regain her voice before she could ask, "Mr. Peterson, do you know where he is?" Simon's kind expression became one of sympathy as he revealed that Tony De Salvo had been deceased for more than sixteen years.

Simon couldn't tell if he saw disappointment or confusion on Chelsea's face. He softly said, "You are probably wondering how he died." When Chelsea shook her head in affirmation he said, "This is what happened. When your grandfather and I realized that both of our daughters had been impregnated by Anthony De Salvo, Theo thought it best if he didn't force the issue. But I was determined to find De Salvo and force him to marry Ellen.

I found him in Cleveland, Ohio, working as a bartender. I brought him back here, and I've regretted that decision ever since. It was the biggest mistake of my life. He started cheating on Ellen right away. In fact, on the day her baby was born, Tony was carrying on with a woman who lived in a second story, walk-up apartment. The woman's husband came home and caught them. He threw De Salvo out the door, and he fell down a long flight of stairs. They took him to the same hospital where Ellen had just given birth to his stillborn son. Tony's body healed, but the fall left him totally blind. Poor Ellen was left with no baby and a mean, bitter husband. It was more than she could take mentally."

Tears began to spill from the old man's eyes. He removed a red handkerchief from his back pocket and dabbed them then said, "A neighbor heard the shots. The police said that Ellen had killed him and then herself."

Familiar, stormy emotions were enveloping Chelsea and they felt just as raw and fresh as they had on the day Simon Peterson told her the truth about the man who fathered her. When she pulled into the driveway and headed for the parking lot behind the church, Chelsea thought about turning around and going home. Suddenly, the dark cloud surrounding her lifted when she was welcomed by a wave from a smiling Haley Applegate.

Chelsea's negative mood changed when she saw the sun gleaming through Haley's red hair. When the two of them stepped inside the church, Haley's brother met them. Bryan Smith said that he had arrived early just so he could sit with them. Chelsea instantly understood that God had brought this church and these two people into her life so that she would be able to find His peace through them. When she sat down in their pew, she thanked Him for being so infinitely merciful and kind.

Chapter 8

Catherine and Lyle Burke were preparing noon dinner together in Whitlock. They were happy to be busy since they had retired from their jobs, and it was all because of James. They both had been under the impression that retirement meant inactivity and boredom. But that was not the case at all! Because James had started a contracting business and was building good quality, modest and affordable single-family homes, the two of them felt useful and needed. His mother was very adept at managing the office along with coordinating deliveries, and his father's expertise at providing estimates regarding building materials and labor costs had already proved invaluable.

Catherine had just set the table when James came into the dining room. She said, "I hope you brought your appetite. We prepared fried chicken and dumplings." His mother had seen a huge difference in her son since his wife's death. She understood the impact that a spouse's death could have on anyone. But considering the unusual circumstances of Margot's death, she thought that James was doing well.

Lyle and Catherine weren't in the least bit surprised when the circumstances surrounding Margot's death became a political hot potato. The police chief in Almeda had already resigned. There was also some question as to whether or not the mayor and judge would each be reelected when their terms expired. Unfortunately, the front page photograph of the politicians grasping an obviously distraught James Burke's hand had aroused suspicions within Almeda's population and that saddened everyone close to the situation.

His parents were thrilled to see their son devour the dinner they had prepared together, but they would surely be disoriented if they could read his mind. He was thinking about how he had been driving that morning on an overpass bridge that crossed above the road to Delite when he caught a glimpse of a red station wagon. He'd quickly turned his truck around to follow but couldn't quite catch up. James finally stopped the chase when he reached a church. From the front parking lot of the church he had read the welcoming sign. He'd noted that the name of the church's pastor was Adam Applegate. Then he'd heard the old hymn, "What A Friend We Have In Jesus", being sung. The familiar melody had caused him to feel nostalgic. He had remembered the times when Kevin and he attended church services together as kids. James was chewing a bite of chicken and thinking that it was very unlikely Chelsea and Sweetie could be anywhere near this area. Then he finally admitted the truth to himself. Chelsea Swanson was still very much in his daily thoughts and nightly dreams.

James thoughts were brought back to the present moment when his father said, "We have so many irons in the fire right now. I'm somewhat concerned that we may have taken on more than we can handle." James said, "I've lined up a crew of six more men. We'll be able to keep up with the work. I'm on top of things." Lyle looked thoughtful as he said, "You've hired more men. Good! So far we've been able to satisfy our clients. We need to keep it that way." James nodded in agreement. Lyle smiled at his son and said, "I've been very pleased with how you've been able to complete the jobs on time and still stay within what's been budgeted. You've done very well, James!"

Catherine had just served the cherry pie with whipped topping when the phone rang. Lyle said that he'd get it, then after a short conversation he returned. His wife took one look at Lyle and could see that he was upset. "What's wrong?" she asked. He said, "Matt Scoggins has died. It happened this morning. He had a heart attack." The three of them sat in silence for a few minutes as they each recalled their own special memories of the Scoggins family. The two families had often vacationed together and the boys had been inseparable until Kevin was killed in the war. Catherine sat staring at the dessert before her and remarked, "Maria shouldn't be alone. I'd better go over there." "We all need to go," said James.

Three days later, Chelsea had the day off from her job at the bank. That morning Haley Applegate called and asked if Chelsea wanted to go to Whitlock with her and Chelsea said yes. Then Chelsea phoned her dad and told him where she was going and that she'd return that afternoon to do her work in the mobile home park. Sam told his daughter to have fun. The two young women met at the church and decided to take Haley's gray Plymouth because she needed to go to the cemetery in Whitlock where her parents were buried and plant some live flowers in the urn at their grave site.

When they arrived at the cemetery, there was a parked funeral procession and an open tent filled with many people. Haley decided to park as far away as possible so they wouldn't disturb the funeral service. After she and Chelsea walked to her parents' gravesite, the two of them immediately began to pull the weeds from around the headstone and plant flowers in the urn. They quickly finished then headed back to Haley's car. Neither of them was aware of the young man standing under the tent who had turned to watch them.

The brightness of the morning sun created a glare on the slow moving, gray car as it drove through the gate at the opposite end of the cemetery. James covered his eyes with his hand and wondered if one of the young women he had seen getting into the car over there could possibly be Chelsea Swanson. But after he thought about it, he knew it wasn't her because Chelsea's hair was much longer and she wouldn't go anywhere without her little bug-eyed dog, Sweetie.

James turned around just as Maria Scoggins was placing one red rose on her husband's coffin. His parents once told him how moved they had been when they saw Maria place a single red rose on Kevin's memorial headstone.

Haley had just driven out through the gate of the cemetery and was feeling comforted by the knowledge that she and Chelsea hadn't intruded on the graveside service that was taking place during their visit to her parents' graves, but Chelsea was thinking something quite different. She was feeling inundated by a strange sense that she couldn't identify. It was almost as if she had just lost something very valuable, but the only thing she had brought with her was her wallet. Chelsea looked down at the wallet she was holding and silently tried to reason why she should be experiencing such unexplainable feelings.

She had turned to look back toward the cemetery when Haley broke into her confusing thoughts by saying, "I don't have very much money, but we can go browsing without buying." Chelsea was feeling a little addled but was able to confess that she was almost broke and thought it would be fun to at least look at what she couldn't afford to buy. The two of them spent what was left of the morning going from shop to shop and then found a quaint cafe. They each ordered a bowl of corn chowder and iced tea for lunch.

During their drive back to Delite, Haley and Chelsea took notice of a new subdivision in Whitlock. They counted at least six homes under construction. Chelsea commented that the housing project took on the air of a park like setting because it sat next to a small lake and had many trees.

Later that day James was admiring the same setting as he visually inspected the six uncompleted homes near the small lake. He was thinking about his folks and their struggle with the upkeep on their present home. He wondered if perhaps a smaller home would be better suited for their needs. James walked over to the two large lots that he had been saving for them and himself and thought that he would soon tell his parents about his idea of building two more homes.

James had sold his home in Almeda and was presently living above his parents' garage in Whitlock. Out of necessity, his business office was located there as well. Although his apartment was cramped, he felt that it had served its purpose well. Even though he hadn't drawn up any plans yet, James could easily imagine his own home with a room that would be used for his office. That room would be just to the left of the front entry hall. In his mind's eye, he could visualize a formal living room that would sit to the right of the entry. He desperately tried to envision a wife and some children, but that image eluded him.

James momentarily watched the waterfowl on the lake then he turned to take another look at the six uncompleted homes. He was pleased with the progress that had been made on them and felt grateful that they had all sold in spite of the fact they weren't yet completed. Just as soon as the six were finished, James could be totally focused on building homes for his parent's and himself.

He looked down at his bleeding palms and said aloud, "Creepin' crud!" The salve that Chelsea Swanson had given him was almost gone. He had stopped using it and the bleeding began all over again. James finally realized that it was time for him to see a doctor.

Saturday night came along fast and Chelsea was getting ready for a date with Bryan Smith. They were going out to dinner. She wondered if it was his idea or his sister's. Haley hadn't been at all discreet when it came to her matchmaking attempts. Chelsea wondered why she wasn't feeling nervous or even a little excited about tonight's date. In fact she hadn't even bothered to take extra care about her appearance. The only makeup she put on was some light pink lipstick. Anyway, she had accepted when Bryan asked her out and he was knocking at her door.

When Chelsea opened the door, Sweetie tried to make an escape. Bryan scooped her up into his arms just in time and said, "Haley and I had a Boston Terrier when we were kids." Chelsea said, "Her name is Sweetie. She belonged to my late mother. I really should walk her. Would you mind if I do that?" she asked. "Sounds good to me." Bryan replied. Chelsea attached the dog's leash and when Bryan asked if he could take it, she handed it over. They followed the excited pooch out the door and the three of them walked toward the beach.

They met up with Sam and Jane while on their way back to Chelsea's trailer. Jane mentioned that she and Sam had made plans for dinner and a movie. When Jane looked into Sam's eyes, he somehow understood that he was to ask if Chelsea and Bryan would like to make it a foursome. Sam was rewarded by Jane for correctly interpreting her unspoken notion when she gave him a cute little smile and a gentle touch on his arm. The younger couple said yes and the evening was pleasurable. Chelsea was pleased that her dad had taken a liking to Bryan.

At the close of their date, Chelsea and Bryan kissed goodnight outside her front door. It wasn't an especially passionate kiss, and Chelsea didn't feel the earth move. But once she got inside her trailer, she had to admit to herself that she had enjoyed being kissed again after such a long time. While lying in bed, the thought occurred to her that perhaps she could never feel a strong emotion for any man ever again. Then James Burke's face popped into her mind. After that thought, Chelsea put in a rather restless night.

As he was driving home, Bryan Smith began to search his mind for the cause of his lack of enthusiasm toward Chelsea Swanson. He came to the obvious conclusion that she is beautiful, intelligent and sweet. But he just couldn't think of anything that would cause him to fall in love with her. He sorely didn't want to face the fact that his one and only true love would always be Margot Burke. That's when he understood that Margot had become like an invasive virus and had permeated his entire being. Bryan had sincerely hoped that by kissing Chelsea's beautiful, pink pouty lips he would finally be free of Margot. But that hadn't happened.

The minute he walked into his home he went straight for the photograph album. He just had to see Margot's face. He had taken her picture at the electric company's fall picnic on the day before she learned that her husband had been wounded in Southeast Asia. That was the last day and night he and Margot spent together. Bryan still dreamed about the love and passion that they had shared that night. He remembered how agonizing it had been for him to see her at work everyday after that. She had even forbidden him from speaking to her unless it was work related. He softly closed the photo album and put it in the bottom desk draw. As he mourned for the love of his life, Bryan Smith realized that this was the loneliest he had ever felt.

The next morning Sweetie needed to go out so she awakened Chelsea before six o'clock. "Who needs an alarm clock with you around?" Chelsea said sleepily. She dressed and they left for their morning walk. They journeyed up and down the streets of the mobile home park and Sweetie greeted her doggy friends. She also decided to be naughty and intimidate three cats before Chelsea pointed her toward home. When they got close to Jane's home, Midnight began to tease Sweetie by darting in and out of the bushes. The white cat would sneak up just out of reach of the leashed dog then run back to conceal himself. The cat's actions caused Chelsea to giggle and she said to Sweetie, "Serves you right!"

When they returned to their trailer, Chelsea saw to Sweetie's needs of food and water then picked up her purse. She would need to have some money ready for the church collection plate this morning. When she reached in to get her billfold, she was dismayed when she pulled out Michael's letter instead. Chelsea read his letter again and sighed. She just hadn't been able to write a reply to him. Her mind tried to conjure up a reasonable excuse so that she could delay what she considered to be an impossible task. But after only a few minutes of dithering, Chelsea sat down to write.

Dear Michael,

Thank you very kindly for your letter explaining the dynamics of your family. It has helped me to understand many things that I was never able to grasp about you and some of your relatives. I'm truly happy that you are doing so well in your new life. I'm doing well also.

I still have feelings for you, but please try to accept that I must decline your offer to get back together with you. Because God has forgiven me, I have been able to forgive you. I want only the best for you and I wouldn't be opposed to us staying in touch with each other through letters.

With prayers,
Chelsea

After Chelsea had written to Michael, she felt grateful that she could at long last understand how it is possible to forgive another person. Although it is an ongoing process, Chelsea understood that with the conscious and repetitive act of humbly praying to God and asking Him to forgive another person's sins as well as our own, He can change our hearts and minds. She thanked God as she folded and placed the letter in the envelope and sealed it. Then, she quickly ate breakfast and showered.

Before she left for church she found Sweetie curled up in the middle of the bed. The dog opened her eyes when Chelsea said good-bye, but didn't move. A smile easily came to her lips at the sight of the lazy doggy.

On her way to church Chelsea drove to the Delite Post Office. She walked in and dropped the letter that she had written to Michael Newton into the mailbox slot. When she turned to leave she thought about James Burke. While walking out of the post office she shook her head and was clueless as to why she would think of him.

She sat with Haley and Bryan during the church service. After that, she and Bryan went for a quick lunch of root beers and hot dogs. Then they went to the afternoon matinee. As they waited in line outside the theater, Chelsea was won over by Bryan's easygoing personality. Even though she enjoyed his company, she felt like something was missing. Once again, she thought of James Burke.

Bryan Smith's former wife, Deidra, was living with her first husband because she really didn't have anywhere else to go. When she asked Vince Chelsea if she could borrow his old, brown pickup truck so she could go to Almeda and buy some groceries, he gladly gave her the keys. Her emotions had been flat until she spotted Bryan with a dark-haired woman standing out in front of Delite's only movie theater. Deidra Smith pulled across the street from him and his new girlfriend and watched them until they walked into the theater. Even though the two of them hadn't been aware that she was so close by, the only thing Deidra wanted to do was shrivel up into a ball and disappear. She couldn't help but be reminded of the times when she had watched Bryan with Margot Burke. Deidra then chided herself for not understanding why she should even care who Bryan was dating. When she finally drove away, she was shaking.

That night Sweetie snuggled with Chelsea in their big bed. Another week lay ahead and Chelsea was really looking forward to it. She remembered how miserable she had been during the month of May in 1968, and was amazed how fast one year had past. Chelsea smiled at the dog and drifted into a pleasant sleep.

The next week seemed to fly by because Chelsea had been so busy. She was exhausted and was looking forward to spending a quiet Friday night alone with her dog. After she got home from her job at the bank, she could only manage to collapse in a chair. As the telephone began to ring, she was thinking of not answering it at the exact moment when she picked up the receiver. Chelsea was rewarded for the effort when the voice of her best girlfriend, Andrea Chambers, chimed in her ear.

Andrea said, "I've got some news to tell you. I'm engaged and you'll never guess who he is!" Andrea paused so Chelsea said, "Well, don't keep me in suspense! Who is he?" Andrea replied, "Asa Wilson!" Andrea giggled when she heard the air expel from her best friend. Then Andrea said, "I know you probably have loads of questions."

That was an understatement. But things became clearer when Andrea filled Chelsea in on all of the details. Andrea explained that not long after Henry Newton passed away Cora began dating John Preston. Chelsea remembered that Mr. Preston had been a good friend of her late father-in-law and that he owned a roofing company. Asa Wilson had told Andrea that Michael's sister, Linda Newton Wilson, and her mother had a falling out over Cora's liaison with Mr. Preston. The two had stopped speaking. Then Andrea told Chelsea that she had just read an announcement in the society column of the newspaper. Cora Newton and John Preston were getting married in June.

But Chelsea was still confused because when she left Meadowview, Asa Wilson was married to Michael's sister. She just had to ask what happened between Asa and Linda. Andrea told her that after Henry's death, Linda took a job as a waitress at the truck stop. There she met and fell in love with a guy who was a regular customer. The last time anyone had spoken to the two of them they were leaving for California to start a new life. Shortly thereafter, Asa got a divorce on the grounds of abandonment. Chelsea could hear the happiness in her voice when Andrea said, "Asa gave me an engagement ring last night."

Then Andrea asked Chelsea, "Now, do you want to hear about Michael?" Chelsea replied, "I know that he went into the Navy because I got a letter from him." Andrea then told her the reason he was in the Navy. Michael had gotten into some trouble with the law and a judge gave him the choice of either joining the Navy or going to jail. Stunned, Chelsea asked, "What did he do?" Andrea told her that the newspaper said Michael had become extremely inebriated and had stolen John Preston's car which he promptly wrecked. It was actually Cora Newton who called the police when that happened.

Chelsea recalled the dozens of times her former mother-in-law had coddled her son instead of allowing his father's intervention after Michael had pulled some stupid stunt. Chelsea softly said, "Michael finally had to stand on his own two feet. It's probably the best thing that his mother ever did for him."

Andrea told Chelsea that Asa moved into the apartment above his garage since it was empty. Andrea said, "It feels a little strange when I see your things in that apartment without you being there. Then again, I get a warm feeling when I'm there." Andrea briefly paused and said, "Asa and I will be living there after we get married. I hope that's alright with you, Chelsea." A very happy Chelsea replied, "I think it's great, Andrea!" After they ended their conversation by promising to stay in touch, Chelsea felt euphoric.

James had tried to find the owner of Teddy Whitefoot, but couldn't. That cat spent most of his time stalking if he was outside or going from window to window if he was inside. But just now the animal yawned lazily and walked to his empty food bowl where he sat down and looked up at James. It was early in the evening and the busy man was going over some figures. Then he noticed that his adopted feline was ready to be fed. James looked back at the cat and said, "It'll be just a few more minutes. I promise!"

After a short time the impatient cat jumped up onto the counter top that sat below the cupboard where his food was kept. When Teddy did that, James thought about setting aside what he was doing, but decided that the spoiled cat wouldn't be unbearably burdened if he had to wait a little longer.

With the paper work finished at last, James stood up and stretched. He felt good about the numbers and knew that his dad would be pleased. Lyle's business advice had been wise. James finally gave some food and fresh water to Teddy. Then he thought that the time had come for him to tell his parents about the two lots he'd been saving for his and their new homes. He hoped that they would be open to his idea.

Chelsea was still feeling tired but couldn't help but be very excited about Andrea's news. She remembered how hard the two of them had worked at stripping and staining some of the old wooden furniture that she'd left in the apartment above Asa's garage. Repairing the old couch with its springs that poked up through the cushions had been a time consuming job. First, they had to screw cork onto the tops of the springs, and then they'd stuffed clean rags and foam over them. It seemed like it had taken forever when they had hand sewn those holes closed. But after all the openings were tightened up, and a dark green slipcover was placed on it, the lumpy old couch looked very nice. Chelsea felt thrilled by the thought of Andrea taking up housekeeping with the furniture that the two of them had worked so hard on together.

Chelsea's happiness for her best girlfriend suddenly gave her a spurt of energy. The dog was only too happy to oblige when Chelsea attached her leash. Sweetie led them to the beach where they found other folks strolling and fishing. The atmosphere was filled with the sights, sounds and smells of the early evening. Neither of them wanted to leave, but the smell of the barbecues and their hungry tummies spurred Chelsea and Sweetie toward home.

While walking back Chelsea said, "We'll have a cookout, Sweetie!" With those words the dog grew very excited and Chelsea was certain the animal understood that there would be some people food in her future. Sweetie began to pull harder, so Chelsea picked her up and carried her for the rest of the way.

Over in Whitlock, Lyle and Catherine Burke were very happy to hear that their son intended to build himself a home in the new addition by the lake. Then they were astonished when he told them that he had saved a lot for them that was right next to his if they wanted it. His father said, "We had the same idea!"

Then his mother asked, "How did you know?" James said, "I've seen you two struggling with the upkeep on this place and thought that you both might be ready for a change." Catherine said, "I'll call a real estate agent in the morning." Lyle nodded and said, "This property is sure to sell. Let's get started on both homes immediately."

Chelsea had just finished grilling the hamburgers when she spotted her dad and Jane walking toward her. The smile turning up the corners of her mouth was genuine when she noticed that they were holding hands. "You're just in time for the picnic," she said. They told her that they'd already eaten but they did take the soda pop she offered them. Jane kept looking at Sam and smiling so Chelsea asked, "What's going on?" Her father said, "We've set a date for our wedding. Keep the third Saturday in June open." Jane added, "It's just going to be a small affair at the church."

Later while Chelsea carried the leftovers and trash from the picnic into her kitchen, she thought about all the good news that she'd received that day. She smiled when she realized that Andrea, Jane and her father had all found something essential to life, and that is love. Because Chelsea didn't want to step on her begging dog, she picked Sweetie up and put her in the kitchen chair next to the window. Chelsea said, "Poor, abused doggy has to settle for watching me finish what I'm doing."

After Chelsea had everything cleaned up, she patted the dog on her head and walked down the hall. She needed to take a shower and get to bed soon because she realized that the next day was going to be physically taxing for her. She would be working until noon in the mobile home park and the afternoon would be devoted to doing whatever volunteer work the Young Adult's Church Group had planned. When she went to bed the dog jumped up right next to her and snuggled. Chelsea yawned and said, "I'm so glad to have you here with me, Sweetie." Then they both fell asleep.

In the same moment that Chelsea and her dog were falling asleep, the visions in James' mind were a harbinger of the thoughts that constantly sabotaged his efforts to control his feelings. His only desire was to be reclaimed from the abyss of sadness into which he had fallen. He knew that in the foreseeable future he would be very busy building the two homes. He also knew that immersing himself in work couldn't make his heart any less hollow. Trying mightily to disconnect himself from his emotions wasn't enough to prevent James from his perpetual agonizing over Kevin and Margot's deaths or Chelsea Swanson's whereabouts. He heard his own voice echo when he spoke Chelsea's name. Teddy came to him, looked up and meowed loudly as if to say, "I'm not her, but I'm here for you now!" Later the cat curled up next to him in their bed and James felt comforted enough to fall asleep.

On the following morning Chelsea did many maintenance chores in the mobile home park and was feeling the effects from at least one of them. She massaged the soreness in her back that she'd gotten from helping her dad lift the push mover into the bed of his pickup truck so that he could take it to the repair shop in Almeda that afternoon. Even though she was feeling a little light headed because she hadn't taken the time to eat, she quickly showered and washed her hair. She didn't want to be late for whatever work the Young Adult's Church Group had planned. She saw to Sweetie's needs then hurried off.

Bryan Smith arrived early at the church's event hall and unrolled the plan to refurbish the community sports park that he had drawn up. He'd spent many fun times as a boy there, and it grieved him that the park had fallen into such a bad state of disrepair. He placed the plan on one of the large tables because he thought he should go over it just one more time. Although he wasn't a professional, he hoped that his drawing would appear at least doable to the other members of the group, especially since his brother-in-law had agreed to present it to them that afternoon.

When Bryan heard his name being called by Adam Applegate, he looked up just in time to see that Chelsea had blood running down her face. He ran over to her then caught her when she fainted. He gently laid her on the floor before someone gave him a cool, damp cloth. When he dabbed her forehead, he found a gash. Haley leaned over them and said, "That's going to need stitches."

Chelsea came to and told them that while she was driving she felt lightheaded. She wasn't sure what happened after that but did remember being on the ground along the side of the road and seeing her car on fire. Then a very nice lady helped her get into a brown pickup truck and brought her to the church. The kind stranger had even helped her walk into the event hall. Chelsea weakly asked, "Where is she?" Then she passed out again.

Chapter 9

Sam and the insurance claim agent were in total agreement. Chelsea's charred station wagon could only be junked. And Chelsea accepted the fact that the accident had been of her own making because she had neglected to eat. She vowed to never let something like that happen again, ever! Sam told the claim agent that his daughter had a mild concussion, but as soon as she was physically able they would begin searching for a replacement car.

After a week of being fussed over by Jane, Bryan and her dad, Chelsea was eager to get back into her regular routine. Bryan had insisted that he should drive her to this morning's church service. She was happy to be going and was very anxious for everyone in the church to see that she was doing fine.

As for Sweetie, she couldn't be happier. Sam and Jane had been spending more than enough time spoiling her. As the dog walked by, Chelsea touched Sweetie on one of her ears and the animal responded by snorting and jumping up to sit next to her. Then she moved as close to Chelsea as she possibly could. Chelsea knew it the moment Bryan's car pulled into her driveway. Sweetie leaped down and stood looking at the door. She had developed affection for the man and no longer barked whenever he came to their home. The two humans patted the dog, and then Bryan slipped his arm around Chelsea's waist and helped her out the door.

Before the church service started, Bryan invited Chelsea, Sam and Jane to come to his home for a barbecue that afternoon. Haley, who had been spying, overheard their conversation and finagled an invitation out of her brother for Adam and herself. Bryan laughed because he found humor in his sister's attempt at intrigue.

When church was over, Sam and Jane went to Chelsea's trailer to get Sweetie. After they arrived at the barbecue, the dog immediately ran to Bryan. Chelsea watched her dog for a few moments and thought she had ulterior motives. Sweetie's behavior was giving away what she was really doing. The dog was constantly sniffing the aromas of the grilling hot dogs and hamburgers as they wafted their way into her nostrils. Bryan grinned as he looked down at the pooch and said, "I know what you're up to."

A little later Jane noticed that Chelsea was sitting quietly with tears in her eyes. Jane touched Chelsea's shoulder and asked, "Is everything alright?" Chelsea smiled and said, "I'm fine. I was just thinking how kind and gracious everyone has been to me since my car accident." She paused then added, "I'm overwhelmed by all the blessings I've received." When she spoke those words, Jane gave her a big hug.

Nobody at the barbecue in Bryan's backyard was aware they were being watched. Deidra Smith craned her neck to try and get a clearer view. From the smells, she instantly knew that Bryan was having one of his famous barbecues. When Deidra saw Bryan's dark-haired girlfriend, a feeling of relief poured over her. Deep down Deidra hoped that her own quick actions on the day of the woman's car accident were at least part of the reason why his girlfriend seemed to be doing so well. Although Deidra hadn't had the courage to face Bryan by walking into the church with the young woman, she had waited around just long enough to make sure that his girlfriend received the help that she needed.

Deidra smiled warmly when Haley and Adam Applegate came into her view, but she didn't recognize the older couple. Then she spotted a Boston Terrier and wondered if Bryan had acquired a dog. Deidra remembered that Bryan told her that he and Haley had that breed of dog when they were kids. She finally drove away with that familiar knot in her stomach that she always got when she knew that Bryan was with Margot Burke. She was really making an effort to stop dwelling on her past with him, but wasn't able to do that, yet.

The third week of June crept up on Chelsea and she still hadn't even bought a dress for what had to be the most important day of her father's life. At last he would be married to a woman who would truly love him!

As she and Haley walked up and down the aisles of the dress store, Chelsea mumbled to herself, "I shouldn't have waited until the week of the wedding to buy a dress." The quiet remark brought a smile to Haley's lips because she knew Chelsea didn't mean for her to overhear it. Just then Chelsea held up two identical dresses she had lifted from the rack. One was yellow and the other was lavender. She asked her friend, "What do you think of these two?" Chelsea quickly replaced them and ran to get a closer look at the dress that Haley had lifted from the rack. "Oh! It's lovely! This is the one!" said Chelsea.

On the day of the wedding Haley was feeling very pleased with herself because Bryan would be wearing the tie that she bought for him. It was the exact shade of mint green as Chelsea's dress. In Haley's mind the two of them seemed perfect together. Bryan, however, felt his sister was pushing just a little bit too hard.

That same day Deidra Smith was obsessively driving past Bryan's apartment in Vince Chelsea's old, brown truck. She spotted him when he came out and got into his car. She wondered why he was wearing his best suit and decided to follow him. Deidra was surprised when he drove to Adam Applegate's church. After he parked, she watched him walk over to greet his new girlfriend with a kiss and that's when she noticed he was wearing a green tie that was the exact same hue as his girlfriend's dress. She thought that it had to be intentional. Suddenly, the thought occurred to Deidra that this was possibly to be the couple's wedding day. She couldn't understand why that thought didn't make her feel more dejected. Was she getting over him? She sincerely hoped that was happening.

Even so, Deidra felt compelled to pull the truck behind some trees that sat across from the church. Then she took the binoculars from the glove compartment and got out. She crawled behind some foliage and crouched down so that she would be hidden. Doing that reminded her of the countless nights she had crawled out through her bedroom window when she was a little girl, so she could hide from her father. He often came home very late and very drunk. When he couldn't find her, he would curse a few times before staggering into his own bedroom and falling on his bed. She always stayed hidden until she could hear him snoring. Knowing it was then safe, she'd sneak back into her own bedroom.

Deidra shivered and deliberately tried to remove those desperate thoughts from her mind. She needed to concentrate on adjusting the binoculars she was holding. By the time she could see through them clearly, Bryan and his girlfriend were nowhere in sight. Then she spotted Vince Chelsea's parents drive into the church's parking lot and go into the church. She couldn't imagine why Joe and Judy Chelsea were there. After a few more people showed up, the front door was closed.

Deidra waited for about thirty-five minutes then the church door opened. Once everyone was outside she could see that photographs were being taken of an older man and woman. Although she didn't know them, she did recognize them. When she had been spying on Bryan, she had seen them in his backyard at his barbecue. It was obvious that they were the couple who had just gotten married. Deidra felt puzzled as she watched Vince Chelsea's parents walk over to the newly married couple and congratulate them. That's when Deidra decided that it was time to get back to Vince.

Chelsea snapped a few more wedding pictures outside the church then hugged Jane and her father before they drove away. She went back inside the church to help with the cleanup. While working she thanked God for bringing someone into her dad's life who would truly return his love.

The church was looking spic and span again, so Bryan walked Chelsea to her new car and placed the half eaten wedding cake on the front seat. Then the two of them kissed. On her way home, Chelsea wanted to think that their kiss had rung the church bells, but she had to face the fact that it hadn't. She shook her head and realized that she didn't want to think that she would never again feel a connection to any man except James Burke.

The week following her father's marriage went by very fast for Chelsea. She came out of the grocery store on that Friday night and smiled when she thought of her father and his new wife. She wanted to have some fresh food waiting for them when they returned the next day. Confusion as to where she had parked overtook her until she remembered that she no longer had her red station wagon. The light, blue Chevy sedan was a lovely car, but she still missed that red, Ford station wagon.

When she reached the mobile home park, Chelsea drove to Jane's and her father's home. She found Midnight outside on the porch curled up on one of the soft cushions of the glider. The white cat had become quite smitten with Chelsea during recent days because he had been fed, watered and lavishly pampered by the young woman. With the exception of the scent from that wild dog of hers, the cat was very pleased to have Chelsea's attention. The fact that Midnight had repeatedly left his scent on her by wrapping himself around her ankles hadn't gone unnoticed by Chelsea, or Sweetie, for that matter.

While driving through that same mobile home park, Catherine Burke set aside the map that her husband had drawn for her and James. Finding the exact street where Maria Scoggin's new trailer was located had been a cinch. From inside the cab of James truck, Catherine and James looked down the street and spotted Lyle. They pulled into the driveway just as Lyle was lifting the last box out of the bed of his truck. It wasn't long before James' truck was also emptied. Maria invited them into the trailer and they sat down in her new home. She served them iced tea. Tearfully, a grateful Maria thanked the Burke family for all that they had done to help her get settled in her new home. Then Maria softly said, "I couldn't have gotten through the last few months without all of you. Thank you."

Chelsea pulled her blue Chevy sedan into her driveway right next to Maria Scoggin's new home. Before their wedding, Jane and her father told Chelsea that they rented the lot next to hers to a widow woman. Chelsea wanted to meet the lady, but saw two trucks sitting in the driveway over there. When her eyes locked onto the newer, green Dodge pickup, she inexplicably felt as though she had found something that she'd lost. She shook her head to discard that strange feeling because she was exhausted and didn't think she should intrude on her new neighbor. Telling herself that it would be best to wait until the next morning, she turned and walked toward her trailer.

Once Chelsea was inside she decided to take a quick shower while she still had the strength. Because Sweetie had seen James go into the trailer next door, she tried immediately to get Chelsea 's attention. The dog yipped and jumped into the chair next to the kitchen window, but Chelsea paid her no mind and walked straight back to the bathroom and got in the shower. After what seemed like an eternity to Sweetie, the dog watched in despair when Chelsea emerged from the bathroom and flopped down into one of the living room chairs.

When James and his parents came out of the trailer next door, Sweetie started barking. Then she began to run back and forth between the chair next to the kitchen window and the chair where Chelsea was seated. Even though Chelsea felt completely fatigued, she finally got up and went over to look out. By the time she got to the kitchen window, Chelsea couldn't see anything really exciting happening. The only thing she saw were the two pickup trucks that had been parked next door heading down the street. Chelsea reached down and gently patted Sweetie on her head and went back into the living room where she once again collapsed in a chair. That left the poor, exasperated little doggy to sit in the chair next to the kitchen window and longingly look out, all alone.

The next morning Chelsea was awakened by her dog. After she saw to Sweeties' needs and got dressed, Chelsea went over to the trailer next to hers and introduced herself to her new neighbor. The woman graciously invited her into the brand new mobile home and told Chelsea that her name was Maria Scoggins. Chelsea had a faint recollection of having heard the woman's last name before but couldn't remember when or where.

Chelsea stepped into the living room and told Maria that her home was quite lovely, so Maria offered to show her the rest of the trailer. When they entered Maria's bedroom, Chelsea was immediately startled by one of the old photographs that was sitting on Maria's dresser. Chelsea's new neighbor pointed to a hand crocheted afghan on her bed and said that it had been made by her mother. Chelsea truly admired the loveliness of the afghan, but her eyes couldn't help but keep darting back to the photograph. After touring the rest of the home, Chelsea told Maria that she needed to leave because her father and his new bride would be returning from their honeymoon and she was going to go over to their place. She said that she wanted to do a little light cleaning so they would come home to a fresh smelling home. Maria told her to come again and Chelsea thanked her for showing her around the mobile home. Then Chelsea said that she would visit again. Chelsea could feel herself shaking as she left Maria's home and hoped that Maria didn't notice. Maria thought that Chelsea was a sweet young woman and was pleased to be living right next door to her.

That same morning, Deidra Smith's blue eyes scanned the horizon of the Gulf of Mexico as an ocean wave splashed around her ankles. For the first time since her mother had gone away forever, she felt almost happy.

Although Deidra couldn't understand why, Vince Chelsea still wanted her. She had hurt him badly when she left him for Bryan Smith, but Vince had recently proposed marriage to her and she was going to marry him for the second time. Deidra turned to face him and he was looking at her with those piercing, dark, brown eyes of his. They had always, somehow been able to penetrate the unseen, and unfailing wall that she erected around herself when she was only a small child. Deidra had never failed to masterfully keep the deepest parts of herself hidden from everyone, with the exception of Vince Chelsea.

Vince knew that Deidra still couldn't understand the love that he had always felt for her since the very first moment they looked into each other's eyes when they were small children. The large man, who some would regard as far from handsome, only spoke when he thought that it was absolutely necessary. "It's time for us to leave now, Deidra," he softly said. Then he gently took hold of the small hand of the cute little blond. Deidra looked up at him and felt safe, but still confused, as they slowly walked together to where his old, brown pickup truck was parked. Vince believed that his love for her could truly cover up a multitude of sins. But he was also wise enough to know that because Deidra's heart and mind had been crushed so many times in her short life that she was still unable to grasp what true love really could be.

As Deidra stared out at the passing scenery from inside Vince's brown pickup truck, she tried not to feel nervous about the upcoming luncheon with his family. She knew that they didn't share his feelings for her. In fact, Deidra had always felt an undercurrent of hatred from his sister, Vanessa. Deidra couldn't remember having ever said or done anything to hurt Vanessa and was puzzled as to why Vince's sister had despised her since their childhood.

For the time being Deidra was feeling comforted by her betrothed's few but very powerful words. She had seen the love in his eyes when he said, "My family doesn't know what I know about you, Deidra. You aren't marrying them, you are marrying me. I promise to spend the rest of my life trying to protect you from ever being hurt again."

Vince's parents and sibling were anticipating the arrival of him and Deidra McClure Smith. His mother, Judy, was preparing a nice lunch in honor of the couple's upcoming marriage. She looked at her husband, Joe, and flatly said, "Vince has a blind spot where Deidra is concerned." Vanessa Chelsea, Vince's older sister, had been sitting quietly in the corner of the living room flipping through the pages of a magazine. She wasn't looking forward to spending even one moment with Deidra and was about to say so when her father said, "Since Vince has asked Deidra to remarry him, let's all try real hard to keep the peace. Let's not be saying or doing anything that will cause her to feel unwelcome." With that comment, Vanessa felt the gall rising in her throat. She wanted to scream and reek havoc in her immediate world, but instead she put on a facade of complete disinterest. While in truth her mind was trying to prepare her for some unknown tragic event that was looming at some point in the future, she was determined to maintain the appearance of calmness just as she had always been able to do since she was nine years old.

Chelsea Swanson had earlier made a polite escape from Maria Scoggin's lovely mobile home. When she arrived at Jane's and her father's place, Midnight followed her into the kitchen. Chelsea saw to the cat's needs of food and water, then dusted and ran the vacuum. Then she sprayed a flower-scented aerosol throughout the mobile home to freshen the air. She was really looking forward to seeing the newlyweds again, for more than one reason. As she drove back to her own home, she decided to tell her father about the photograph that she had seen in Maria's home. Chelsea had no doubt that he could be trusted to guide her as to how to best handle the situation.

That evening Chelsea was changing into her T-shirt and shorts. Sweetie sat quietly on the bed then jumped down to the floor and began to act like a wild doggy. She ran back and forth in the hallway a few times, and then jumped onto a rag rug that slid beneath her. It carried her down the length of the hallway and into the living room. There Sweetie smacked right into the side of a chair and it hurt. She yelped, then immediately ran to Chelsea to get some sympathy. She received it, of course. After a minute, Sweetie didn't need anymore gentle caresses from Chelsea, so her human put a leash on the dog and they walked to the home of the newlyweds.

When they arrived, Chelsea's father had just finished putting lighter fluid on the charcoal in the barbecue. He struck a match and the flames began to dance. Jane thanked her new stepdaughter for the fresh food and good care that Midnight had received. Then she invited Chelsea to stay for the barbecue. The newlyweds said that they were very happy to be home even though their honeymoon had been extremely enjoyable. Chelsea smiled because it was impossible to miss that they were exchanging romantic glances.

While the hamburgers were grilling, they told Chelsea that they were going to purchase another home. They also said that they had decided to get a home that would sit on two lots instead of one. Sam could see the puzzled look on his daughter's face so he explained that the home would come in two halves. He said that when the halves were attached, that it would have a peaked roof. Chelsea was excited and couldn't wait to see what their new home would look like. Sam also said that he would rent his home and Jane told Chelsea that she wanted her trailer to become the new office for the mobile home park.

When Jane went into the trailer to get the condiments, Chelsea mentioned to her dad that she wanted to have a private talk with him in the near future. Seeing the concerned look on her father's face caused her to explain that there wasn't any reason for him to be worried and that she merely wanted to discuss something very personal with him.

That same evening in a different part of Delite, Jack McClure, Deidra's father, stumbled out of a liquor store. The couple who unfortunately found themselves on the same sidewalk with Jack, had to step aside and into the street because he was the source of an overwhelming, offensive stench. That man seemed to reek of alcohol, sweat, urine and every other unpleasant odor known to mankind. For years any other human who had been unlucky enough to come within ten feet of the filthy man, found themselves desperate to get away from him just as fast as they possibly could. Jack staggered back to his old, dilapidated car and crawled in. He carefully placed the booze, which he always referred to as his treasure, on the car seat and began to drive back to the disgusting hovel where he lived.

Deidra couldn't believe that she and Vince had spent the entire day with his family. Judy Chelsea had put on a lovely lunch, and then Vince and Deidra helped Joe with the afternoon farm chores. Afterward, Joe asked Vince and her to have supper with them. Judy had actually smiled when her husband asked them. But Vince decided that they needed to get back to his home on the Chelsea ranch. Deidra felt relieved but was still feeling perplexed because Vince's sister, Vanessa, hadn't even made one unkind remark to her. Overall, she thought that the day had been a very nice one until they passed by her father's car while they were heading for home. She supposed that the man had been on a run to get some cheap booze so that he could drink the night away, as was his usual routine.

Vince knew the woman he loved enough to know that she was thinking about her father. He wished that they hadn't driven by the loathsome man while they were going to their home. Vince

Chelsea truly believed that Jack McClure had to be the most despicable human being on the planet.

Earlier that day while driving to his parent's home, Vince had reached for Deidra's hand and she had recoiled. Her entire body had actually gone rigid for a brief moment. Then her demeanor seemed to soften when she looked up at him and smiled. Vince had always felt that he would actually melt whenever she smiled at him.

In this exact moment he couldn't see anything the matter with his blind devotion to the beautiful young woman sitting next to him. His only desire was that his second marriage to her would be enough for Deidra to overcome her self-destructive tendencies. His every thought and prayer was of how he could show the only girl he had ever loved that she needed him and could love him! Then she would be able to get past all the pain that Jack McClure had inflicted on her.

Later the darkness of the night cocooned the two of them in their antique bed. Deidra fell asleep nestled in Vince's arms. His senses were heightened by the sounds of her steady breathing and the sweetness of her occasional sighs. As he held the one and only reason for his existence, his thoughts took him back to the very first time he had looked into her sad blue eyes.

His parents had given him a puppy for his fifth birthday. The dog ran away from him and went into a field near his home. Vince had gotten lost while searching for the puppy and he wandered into an area of the property that was unfamiliar to him. He stumbled and fell into a low-lying, brushy depression in the field. He crawled up and had almost reached the top when he heard footfalls coming toward him. He peered up over the edge and saw a little girl being pushed down. Then he watched as a man tore off her clothes. As a little boy he had felt very frightened even though he hadn't understood what he was witnessing. Somehow he had instinctively known that what was happening to the little girl was very wrong. During the violent act, the little girl didn't scream or even cry. She simply turned her tiny head and looked into Vince's eyes as he helplessly looked into hers. That recollection still caused him to cry. Through his tears he softly whispered, "I love you, Deidra. I've always loved you."

Chapter 10

It was September 1969 and Chelsea Swanson was feeling a little out of kilter. On the previous evening Brian Smith had proposed marriage to her. She told him that she needed some time to think. When she wondered what she needed to think about, the face of James Burke popped into her mind. She shook that thought from her head as she attached the dog leash to Sweetie's collar. The early evening air felt good to Chelsea as the two of them strolled past Maria Scoggin's mobile home. Then the thought of her new neighbor gave Chelsea a warm feeling.

It had been difficult for Chelsea to tell her father about the photograph that she had seen in Maria's bedroom and also where she had seen it before. But just as she had known he would be, Sam Swanson had been very understanding and supportive. He immediately phoned Maria and asked if his daughter and he could speak with her.

After Sam explained why they were there, Maria had opened up. She began by saying, "Anthony De Salvo was my brother." Although many years had past, she still became misty-eyed whenever she spoke of him. "Tony was the best older brother that a girl could have ever wanted. When we were kids in Cleveland, Ohio, we used to go down to the public beach and swim in Lake Erie. He always bought me popcorn. But the memory that I cherish the most is of Tony bringing home soda pop every Friday night." Maria then explained that after Tony graduated from high school, he had gone to work for the Sunset Bottling Company in Cleveland.

She continued. "When World War II came along, he signed up to fight for his country. During the Battle of the Bulge, poor Tony received a head wound. He was hospitalized for several months. After he came home, our family saw a change in him. He was no longer the kind and generous Tony that everyone had known and loved. The traumatic head wound caused him to become mean. When he moved away, we didn't hear from him for a while. Then out of the blue he called us and said that he was going to be married. We were all very excited and happy to be attending his wedding in Buffalo, New York. But the marriage was troubled." Maria had looked down at the picture in her hands which happened to be the same picture that Chelsea had seen in Simon Peterson's office years earlier.

Chelsea and Sam were both moved by the tears that were spilling from Maria's eyes. Chelsea had touched Maria's arm and said, "You needn't continue, Maria. I already know what happened. Ellen Peterson's father told me a few years ago when I tried to find my birth father. I'm pretty sure that your brother, Tony, is my natural father."

Sam had invited Chelsea and her biological aunt to dinner. He was very happy the two of them had found each other, but also knew that they both needed some time to adjust to their blood kinship. Sam sincerely hoped he could help them do that. Jane had put it best when she said, "All of our lives have been enriched because you two have at last been brought together."

Maria thought that it was nothing short of miraculous that they had finally met. She said, "Our family had always known about you and we wondered if you would ever look for us. We didn't exactly know where to find you." She paused then said, "Tony told us that he had impregnated two women at the same time. Ellen Peterson was the one that he was forced to marry. We knew the other woman's name was Darlene Langston, but that was all he would tell us about her."

Chelsea marveled because she never even knew that she had an aunt. While they were cleaning up after dinner, Maria asked Chelsea if she wanted to call her Aunt Maria. Chelsea had looked to her dad. Sam was smiling when he said, "All our hearts are large enough to make room for your Aunt Maria." Then Chelsea had given each of the other three a hug beginning with her dad. When she hugged Maria, Chelsea said, "I'm glad we found each other, Aunt Maria."

While they had been eating their dessert of vanilla ice cream topped with chocolate syrup, Maria told all of them that she would be happy to show them her De Salvo/Scoggins photograph albums. Not wanting to be pushy, Maria emphasized that it depended on when Chelsea was ready to look through them.

As Chelsea and the dog continued walking, her thoughts were brought back to the present when Sweetie tugged hard on her leash. The stray cat that the dog had spotted scampered out of sight. When Chelsea decided that they had walked far enough, she coaxed the dog back toward their mobile home. Unexpectedly, Sweetie stopped when they turned onto the street where they lived. The dog growled softly and seemed reluctant to keep heading for home. Chelsea assumed that another animal was in the vicinity and didn't pay any attention to Sweetie's actions.

As they neared their trailer, through the dim light Chelsea was able to make out the figure of someone sitting on one of her lawn chairs. She heard the words, "Hello Chelsea," and stopped dead in her tracks. Being well acquainted with his rich masculine voice she asked, "Michael! What are you doing here?"

Catherine Burke was finishing her nightly routine when she said, "I'll only be another moment, Lyle. I'm putting on some hand lotion before I get into bed." This was Lyle and Catherine's very first night in their brand new home. They had intended to move into the home earlier, but James and his crew had been very busy building other homes during the summer months. With their finances and business in order, Catherine thought that things couldn't be better for the Burke family.

James was stretched out on a bed just down the hall from his parent's bedroom. He felt fortunate to be staying with them for the time being because his home wasn't yet livable. As he stared up at the freshly painted ceiling, he realized that the exhaustion that had been incessantly hounding him was now commonplace. James knew that if it wasn't for the very strong, black coffee that he seemed to be consuming more and more of, he wouldn't even be able to drag himself through a day. He looked over at his alarm clock and it was almost midnight.

Back at Chelsea's home, she had fed Michael and tried to make him feel as comfortable as could be on her couch. She wondered if she would even get a wink of sleep as she picked up her alarm clock. It read exactly midnight. She set it for five o'clock then rolled over. As she began to mull over the promise she had made to her former husband, she questioned whether or not what she had decided to do for him was wise. She had told him that she would drive him up to Pensacola. He had said, "I'll be attending an abbreviated photography school, compliments of the United States Navy."

"What have I gotten myself into?" she silently asked herself. Chelsea thought about the earlier phone call she had made to her father. She told him that she wouldn't be able to work in the mobile home park the next day. He hadn't asked her for an explanation and for that she was very grateful. Then she wondered how he could possibly understand why she was doing a favor for Michael when she couldn't understand it herself.

On the next morning the event that had taken place was very low keyed. The former, Mrs. Bryan Smith, was once again Mrs. Vince Chelsea. The simple civil ceremony at the county courthouse was far more preferable to Deidra and Vince than a church affair. And this time around she was determined to be the kind of wife that the man she was preparing lunch for deserved.

Deidra finished making her husband's tuna salad sandwich and remembered the day Vince unexpectedly showed up at her and Bryan Smith's front door just a few weeks after Margot Burke had been killed. Vince told her that he knew her well enough to know that she hadn't taken that woman's life on purpose. Unfortunately, Vince was still standing outside their front door when Bryan came home. Vince quickly left and she tried to explain to Bryan that she hadn't invited Vince Chelsea, but Bryan was very angry and refused to believe her. He told her to her face that he didn't trust her. Those words had crushed Deidra. After she had tossed and turned all that night while agonizing over Bryan's unfaithfulness with Margot Burke and his accusations of her own infidelity, she decided to ask for help from the only person she knew she could trust. Within an hour Vince came and got her.

She looked up just as Vince came in from the barn. He was washing up for lunch at the kitchen sink when Deidra walked up behind him and wrapped her arms around his large waist. Then she said, "You're the only person I've ever been able to depend on." He turned and playfully tried to wipe his wet hands on her blouse, but soon the teasing was replaced with passion as he began to kiss her. At that moment, Deidra McClure Chelsea felt more loved and protected than she had ever been during her entire life.

Later that same morning, Chelsea and Michael were on their way to Pensacola. He said, "Considering what I put you through, it sure is nice of you to drive me to my Navy school. You really didn't have to do this, but I'm very glad that you did. Thank you." Chelsea hadn't said much for most of the trip because she had been finding it hard to believe the changes in her former husband. He had never, ever thanked her for anything before. It was as though Michael Newton had become a totally different person altogether.

As they traveled, Michael explained that he had attended a four-month school in Colorado and that he and the other men in his group had all been specially chosen for it. He was rather proud of the fact that he had learned in that school to find his position on the ground by surveying his surroundings and then matching them up to a spot on a topographical map. He said, "Next I'll spend a week in that abbreviated photography school I told you about." Then he told her that some of the schools were necessarily shortened because the skills that he and the others in his group were learning were vital for the war effort. He also mentioned that some of the men were attending a radio school and a corpsman school. When Chelsea asked him what a person would learn in a corpsman school, he said that a guy could learn how to be a Navy medic. Michael continued, "Our group will be reunited in a two week survival school at Subic Bay in the Philippines." Chelsea was struck by the fact that Michael seemed to be very excited about his naval service. She couldn't remember having ever seen him this devoted to such a worthwhile endeavor.

When they neared the Pensacola Naval Air Station it was almost noon. Suddenly Michael became serious. He turned to Chelsea and began apologizing for all of the unkind and sarcastic things he had said to her and told her that he deeply regretted neglecting her instead of giving her the love and attention that she deserved. After she drove into a parking space along the street Michael said, "I'm honestly ashamed of my infidelity, Chelsea." Then he pulled an envelope from his shirt pocket and said, "Thank you for this letter that says you have forgiven me."

She would have started crying if Michael hadn't pointed and said, "Over there is a sign for a shuttle bus." They both looked toward the sign, then at each other. They leaned into one another and kissed. It was a truly sweet and loving kiss. Then he spoke softly as he said, "Thanks for everything, Chelsea. You're not like any other person I've ever known."

They both heard then saw the shuttle bus in the same moment. After Michael opened the passenger door he kissed Chelsea on her cheek before saying, "I guess that it's a Navy thing, but I'll say good-bye the way my instructors in Colorado did." With his eyes full of expression and the volume of his voice very low he said, "Quack, quack! Quack, quack, quack!

Chelsea watched Michael run to catch the shuttle bus and didn't realize that she was staring after him with her mouth open. Then she could see him waving through one of the bus windows. She waved back and noticed that her hand was trembling. As the bus pulled away and went out of her sight, the knowledge that Michael was training to become like the men who James Burke encountered in Southeast Asia settled deeply into Chelsea's mind.

At that moment on the Chelsea ranch, Deidra thought that the noise in the pig barn was almost deafening, but she didn't mind. She was in love with everything about the cute, little squealing piglets. Finally, she was beginning to feel at ease in her daily life because of Vince's unconditional love. She stepped outside and looked up into the September blue sky and watched the puffy white clouds floating overhead. She hadn't felt this carefree since before her mother went away just a few days after Deidra's fifth birthday.

Vince watched and thought his wife seemed to be skipping back toward their house to fix his lunch. He had made a special point of insisting to his father that they should raise some hogs on the Chelsea ranch. Although the beef cattle were the mainstay of their business, Vince knew that Deidra had a special affection for baby pigs. He smiled at the thought of how her face just seemed to light up when she held one of the little guys.

That night in the Burke home Catherine awakened Lyle. He immediately heard his son crying out in the bedroom down the hall. By the time his parents got to him, James had positioned himself on the edge of the bed. He was just about to fall off. He woke up and caught himself. His concerned parents could see the sweat dripping from his forehead. Lyle helped his son sit up while his mother ran to get a damp facecloth. By the time she returned, James was awake and feeling embarrassed.

The scared looks on both of their faces made him feel terrible. James said he was sorry and explained that his bad dreams had become more frequent since last April when he thought he had seen Chelsea Swanson's red station wagon. Neither of them knew what he was talking about and asked simultaneously, "Who's Chelsea Swanson?"

James knew he needed to help his parents understand what was happening to him so he decided to tell them everything from the beginning. He told them all that happened to him when he was overseas. Although he had already told them about some of the situations that he had been in, this time he really opened up. Reliving Kevin's death was the low point for all of them. When he spoke about the men who had rescued him, his parents paid very close attention. Lyle thought that the quacking sound the men made as they parted company was very unusual and interesting. The other two could almost see the wheels turning in Lyle's head as he pondered it.

Finally Catherine said, "But you never told us who Chelsea Swanson is." Lyle and Catherine had known that there had been a problem between their son and his wife before her death, but he had never told them that she had confessed to having had an affair when he was overseas. They were both shocked when he confided that. He said, "The night she told me about it, I left. It took me awhile to cool down. Finally I decided to come home and try to work things out with Margot." Then he paused and said, "But before I came to that conclusion, I met

Chelsea Swanson in Spruce Pine, North Carolina. She almost ran over me!"

James related to his parents every detail of the relationship that developed between Chelsea and him. He also told them about her Boston Terrier, Sweetie. By the time he had finished, it was beginning to get light outside. James apologized for keeping them up for most of the night, but Lyle waived his hand and said, "You have no need to apologize, James." Then his mother said, "I hope by telling us these things that you'll be able to sleep easier from now on." Then she gave him a hug like only a mother can give.

Lyle asked the other two if they would like a cup of his strongly brewed coffee and they both gave him an affirmative nod. They all enjoyed its aroma as it percolated and were grateful when the dark brown liquid was finally poured into their waiting cups. While they all sat around the table sipping the great smelling and tasting beverage Catherine suddenly said, "James, I think you might be in love with Chelsea Swanson." James remained silent as he stared down at his coffee cup.

Two days later Chelsea Swanson thought that Sweetie needed to get outdoors and enjoy the early morning air. The dog was full of energy. It seemed as though Sweetie was having just too much fun as she jumped high to catch the red, bouncing ball that Chelsea threw. After playing for about ten minutes the dog seemed to show less enthusiasm for the game, so Chelsea picked her up and carried her into their trailer. Then she made sure that Sweetie had plenty of food and water before leaving for the park's office.

Chelsea was wondering what kind of work her father had planned for the day as she walked by Jane's and her father's beautiful, new double-wide mobile home. She approached the park's new office and said hello to Midnight. The white cat was sitting on the front step of where he used to live with Jane. Chelsea was feeling a little sorry for the confused cat when her father came out and handed her a small list of things that she would be doing. Before he turned to leave, Chelsea touched his arm and told him that she needed to speak with him. He said, "I think I know what you want to talk about. I saw Michael three days ago walking up towards your trailer. I noticed that he was carrying his Navy sea bag. At the time I thought it would be best if I just minded my own business. The next morning I watched your car drive by and he was sitting in the passenger seat."

Chelsea was smiling as she explained that she had driven her former husband to Pensacola so he could get some additional training from the U. S. Navy. Then she told her father that Michael had finally become a very responsible person. She said, "I can now respect him and realize that anyone can change if they'll just try." When Chelsea thanked her father for honoring her privacy, Sam was glad that he had done the right thing by not intervening and letting his daughter make her own life decision.

On that same morning Deidra was hanging some new curtains in her and Vince's bedroom. Suddenly, through the open window she could hear her mother-in-law screaming. She ran outside toward the sound of Judy Chelsea's wails and saw Vince's sister, Vanessa, running toward the hay barn. By the time they both reached Judy, they saw that the tractor had tipped over and she was pinned between the tractor and barn.

Vanessa yelled to Deidra that she was going back to phone for help just as Joe and Vince were returning from doing their morning cattle feeding chores. When the men saw what was happening, Joe immediately ran to his wife. Vince jumped down from the tractor seat and disconnected the hay wagon. Then he got back up on the tractor and pulled close to the tractor that had his mother pinned before attaching a cable between the two tractors. Vince quickly got back up on his tractor and put it in reverse. When Judy was freed she collapsed into her husband's arms and passed out.

An ambulance soon arrived and the Chelsea family followed it to the hospital. After anxiously waiting outside the emergency room, they were all relieved to hear from Dr. Carl Morse that Judy probably hadn't sustained any serious injuries. However, as a precaution, he had ordered some x-rays. Joe asked to see his wife and Dr. Morse motioned for him to follow. Joe felt relieved when he found Judy joking with the attending nurse about how it hadn't been a very good idea for her to leave the tractor in gear before walking in front of it. Soon an orderly came to take her to get those x-rays and she was helped into a wheelchair. Joe bent down and gave his wife a kiss before going back to where the rest of his family was waiting. About a half hour later, Judy was wheeled back to her family and they went home.

That evening, Vanessa opened two cans of chicken noodle soup for supper. She cut up some small pieces of cheese while the soup was heating on the stove. After making up two trays of soup, crackers and cheese, she took them into the living room where her parents were sitting. By the time her father realized that Vanessa hadn't brought in any food for herself, she was already walking up the creaky wooden stairs toward the bedroom that had been hers since the day she was born. She heard her father ask, "Has Vanessa already eaten?" Then she heard her mother say in a flat voice, "Just let her go. She's in another one of her moods."

Joe and Judy Chelsea would have eaten in total silence if not for the noisy television. When they were finished, he took both trays back into the kitchen and began to clean up. Judy decided that she would feel more comfortable if she could sit in the soft, winged-back chair next to the window.

After she sat down, Judy looked outside and saw a bolt of lightning brighten the sky in the direction of Jack McClure's place. Afterwards her mind was unable to distinguish any of the sounds that the television seemed to be droning. That noise brought forth distant memories that Judy had never been able to drive deep down into her psyche. As if those memories had a will of their own, she recalled that back when her husband was young he had worked tirelessly on their cattle ranch. With only the company of Vanessa and Vince, Judy had become restless. Then one day she went for a walk and saw two men repairing a fence on the adjoining property that her husband's grandparents owned. She recognized her grandfather-in-law, Nathan Chelsea, instantly. Judy walked over to say hello to him. Nathan had introduced her to his new employee, Jack McClure.

Judy remembered trying very hard not to watch the rippling muscles in Jack's tanned arms each time he pulled on the fence before nailing it to the post. When he took off his ball cap, a full head of wavy, light, blond hair was revealed. Then she made the mistake of looking into those intense blue eyes of his. They seemed to seize her, then hold her captive within them. Judy had understood instantly that she needed to escape. She quickly excused herself and retreated for fear of making a fool of herself. As she was walking away, neither Judy Chelsea nor Nathan Chelsea realized that Jack McClure had been discretely taking in all of her during the entire time of their encounter.

While her mother was downstairs reminiscing, Vanessa was sitting in the upstairs of the Chelsea farmhouse with a large, smoky gray cat curled up on her lap. Izzy's purring let Vanessa know that he was enjoying the slow, back and forth motion of the rocking chair they were sharing. The young woman gazed out through her bedroom window while raindrops rolled down and distorted her view. Unfortunately the movement of the water on the blurred glass reminded Vanessa of the worst day of her life. She desperately wanted those horrible memories to vanish, but the sights and sounds of that day were promptly absorbed throughout her mind and they coerced her into their midst.

When Vanessa was nine years old, her mother had gone for a walk during a light rain shower. Vanessa thought it was odd for her mother to go walking in the rain, so out of innocent curiosity she followed. Vanessa was soaking wet by the time she reached the old shack down by the creek and couldn't understand why her mother had gone there. She was even more puzzled when their neighbor, Jack McClure, showed up.

After her mother and Jack went in the shack, Vanessa wanted to see what was happening so she walked around to the other side and peered through a window. Although the glass had been wet and the images blurred, she had seen her mother and their neighbor partly undressed. As if that wasn't shocking enough, Vanessa saw Mrs. McClure come crashing though the door and slap her mother in the face. Jack McClure had stepped between the two women and grabbed his wife's arms. Next Vanessa watched in horror as her mother picked up an old board and hit Vicky McClure over the head with it.

The woman's scream still echoed in Vanessa's mind which caused her to cringe. The disturbed cat momentarily stopped its rhythmic series of low purrs until Vanessa assured him with a few gentle strokes across his back. During the sleepless hours that followed, Vanessa listened to the falling raindrops while repeatedly envisioning the horrific scene of that day. Jack had cried out, "Vicky's dead. You've killed her!" Then Vanessa saw her mother take a filthy tarp from the corner of the shack and wrap Vicky's body in it. What happened after that was unknown to Vanessa, because she had run all the way home to the safety of her bedroom.

Keeping the secret of what she had witnessed that day for all these years had prevented Vanessa from ever having any sort of close relationship. The only way that she could cope with daily life was to immerse herself in farm work. Vanessa had no desire to socialize and in fact, she preferred the company of her cat or any other animal over any human being.

On the other side of the Chelsea ranch, Vince was awakened from a sound sleep. His wife had cried out, so he gently roused her. When Deidra was awake enough to be aware of her safe surroundings, she assured her husband that she was fine. After a few minutes she could tell by his smoothly paced breathing that he had fallen back to sleep. But Deidra knew that she wouldn't fall asleep so easily because of the nightmare she'd had about her father.

On countless occasions the man came home after drinking away half the night. He was always muttering incoherently. After consuming even more alcohol, his mumblings would turn into a full-fledged tirade which always began with the words, "Judy and I were in love, but your mother had to go and stick her nose into it! Vicky got what was coming to her. Then we dumped her body way out in the Gulf of Mexico. That's right! She got what was coming to her!"

While Deidra was growing up she had always thought that her father's drunken ramblings were unreliable and often questioned what she had done that caused her mother to leave. But now that she was an adult she began to consider the possibility that his many confessions of dumping her mother's body out in the Gulf might be true. She also wondered why he

114

had always used the word, we, when he spoke about disposing of her mother's body. That meant he must have had help. And who was the Judy that he always talked about? The only Judy she knew was her mother-in-law. Deidra was certain that Judy Chelsea could never take part in getting rid of a body.

Chapter 11

Earlier in the year Sam had suggested to Chelsea that her mobile home's roof should be coated so it wouldn't develop a leak. That one simple project started a cascade of remodels. Chelsea had new windows, white aluminum siding, and a screened in front porch added to her home. Just yesterday she had a metal awning connected to the back of the trailer. Before Chelsea drove away she had to admire the appearance of the place. But then she felt a little unnerved when she remembered where she was going and why.

Chelsea had been unprepared for Bryan Smith's marriage proposal, and if she had to be honest with herself she would much prefer that he hadn't asked. Even though he was quite handsome and very, very nice, she just couldn't think of him as being anything but a good friend. Sadly, Chelsea had to face the fact that she had fallen in love with James Burke during the short time they spent together. That realization truly grieved her because he was married.

Apprehension wanted to take control of Chelsea's essence, but the knowledge of God's abiding love strengthened her as she pulled her car into one of the parking spaces next to Bryan Smith's apartment building. After she got out of the car, the evening air felt good on her face. By the time she reached Bryan's front door she hesitated and thought how the evening would be much easier for her if he just didn't answer when she knocked. Then by leaning on the Lord, Chelsea was able to muster up the courage to rap on the door.

It swung open and he greeted her with his engaging smile. Bryan invited her in and because of the puzzled look on his face Chelsea could tell that he was wondering why she was there. She decided that it would be best if she got straight to the point and tell him that she couldn't accept his marriage proposal. She blurted out what she had to say and was surprised by his reaction. His smiling eyes told her that he was taking her rejection of him very well. In fact, Bryan Smith actually sounded relieved when he threw his hands up in the air and said, "It's Haley! She thinks we're made for each other!" Chelsea thought for a moment then said, "So, your sister has been pressuring you." She shook her head and said, "I don't think either of us is ready to jump into another marriage." Then she thought of James Burke while Bryan was thinking of Margot Burke. Neither Chelsea nor Bryan wanted to honestly confess the reasons for their unwillingness to marry. But they did agree to end any romantic involvement and replace that with true friendship.

The next morning Joe Chelsea turned on the kitchen radio and tuned it to a local station. He was taken aback when the announcer stated that the dead body of Jack McClure had been found lying on the ground next to his home. Joe jumped when the coffee cup that his wife was holding crashed to the floor and was splintered to smithereens. The stunned pair stood staring at the radio when Vanessa came in from the barn. Seeing their distressed looks she asked, "What's wrong?"

After her mother composed herself she said, "We just heard on the radio that one of our neighbors has been found dead." Vanessa asked, "Who was it?" Joe said, "Jack McClure." That was all Vanessa had to hear. She went right back out and didn't return to the house for the rest of the day.

Later that morning a deputy sheriff came to the Chelsea farm. He found Deidra and her husband in the pig barn. Deputy Jay Stevens spoke softly and with kindness when he told Deidra that he was sorry for her loss. The man watched Deidra cradle a baby pig in her arms then turn around and walk away without saying anything. Vince spoke in almost a whisper when he said, "My wife's still in shock." Then he asked, "What exactly happened to my father-in-law?"

Jay said, "We believe that he was electrocuted by lightning when he tried to change the direction of the pole that holds his television antenna. Lightning was reported in that area last night and he had a wrench in his hand when a neighbor found him on the ground right next to the antenna pole."

That afternoon Vanessa rode her horse, Manny, down to the creek. As she sat atop him, the chestnut colored Morgan horse pawed at the water with its hooves. Vanessa fought to keep her gaze from going to the patch of ground where the musty old shack had once stood, but then she felt as if her eyes were being pulled there by an unseen force. She was helplessly staring at the exact spot and remembering how she had set fire to that horrible structure. Suddenly, Vanessa was unprepared for the overpowering feeling of sadness that came crashing down on her. Why should recalling the drastic act of destroying that dilapidated building cause her to have to grapple with such an unfamiliar emotion? Particularly since she hadn't really been able to feel much of anything except fear and seething anger for so many years.

Her mind pulled her within its whirlpool of bad memories and she recalled being a twelve year old who had become enraged at her mother. For three years the woman had either moped around the house before looking out the living room window toward Jack McClure's place, or she'd gone for long walks down to the shack. One day Vanessa decided she'd had enough.

She remembered that it hadn't been an easy chore for her to lug a completely filled, five gallon can of gasoline down to the shack and splash it over every inch of the inside of that dump. Then after going outside she had thrown in a match. The explosion that resulted when the flame of that match contacted the strong vapors of the gas knocked her down hard. Thinking back, she didn't know how she had escaped being burned or for that matter how she had managed to have enough wits about herself to remember to pick up the gas can.

All those years ago she had run towards home just as fast as she could and stashed that empty can in one of the outbuildings. After that was done she had looked back toward the creek and recalled feeling invigorated because she thought the black, billowing smoke rising from that shack was setting her free. Unfortunately, with time that liberated feeling vanished. Vanessa realized that unlike that old shack, her bad memories had not been obliterated and were still holding her hostage.

Vanessa shook her head in the hope of dislodging those horrible thoughts before she dismounted the horse. She moved around to the front of Manny's long face and nuzzled his big nose with her own, then grabbed his reins. They slowly walked home and finally arrived late in the afternoon. She took Manny into the barn and saw to his needs before going into the house through the back door. There she found her mother on the kitchen telephone. Vanessa wondered with whom she was speaking, then overheard her mother say, "Thank you so much. Jack McClure deserves a decent send off." Not wishing to hear another word, Vanessa retreated to her bedroom just as she had done more times than she dared to count throughout her life.

Two mornings later, Vanessa found herself in the outrageous position of having to argue with her father because she didn't want to go with him and her mother to Jack McClure's funeral. Vanessa respected her father for always attempting to do what he thought was the right thing. But because he did not know about her mother's dalliance with that horrible man, she wasn't able to give him a good reason for not wanting to go with them. Vanessa thought the whole situation was especially ironic since her own brother and Deidra, the daughter of the deceased man, refused to attend. In disbelief, Vanessa stormed up to her bedroom.

Later that same morning, Vanessa, being the ever-dutiful daughter she had always tried to be, attended Jack McClure's funeral. She sat stoically next to her father while not daring to look at her mother or that monster in the coffin. Then she counted eight of Jack McClure's neighbors including her parents and herself. She was trying to think about anything other than her present surroundings and began to reflect on how much she truly enjoyed riding her horse, Manny.

Vanessa didn't realize that the minister had finished the service when her father nudged her in the side. He was already standing when Vanessa looked up at him. Her father nodded toward the mourners who were beginning to file by the casket one last time. Joe started to walk over to the casket, but instead of following her father Vanessa left the room. She headed down the hall, went out of the funeral home and was welcomed by the fresh air as it soothed her with its gentle touches. Still, she was clutched with the sickening feeling of having just participated in the farce of a tribute to Jack McClure's life. Soon all the others came out. It made Vanessa sick to her stomach when her mother tearfully invited everyone who had attended the funeral to her home for a lunch in memory of their neighbor. None accepted with the exception of Janice Potts. Her husband, Wendall, just stood there and gave his wife an unreadable look but said nothing.

During their ride home, Joe Chelsea thought that his wife had to be the most unselfish person he had ever known. She had taken it upon herself to plan a funeral for a man that nobody liked. Joe had even seen tears in Judy's eyes during the funeral service. He felt so proud to have a wife that was as kind as Judy.

When Mr. and Mrs. Potts reached the Chelsea home, Joe already had the coffee made. He hoped that his moody daughter would stick around for a light lunch, but Vanessa quickly changed into her jeans and went out to the horse barn. Joe Chelsea didn't realize that his daughter soon returned and was silently and sullenly helping her mother prepare a tray of ham sandwiches in the kitchen.

The Potts came into the living room and Joe offered Wendall and his wife a seat. Wendall sat down on the couch. But Janice who had already begun the endless running of her mouth, made herself comfortable in the largest chair in the room. Not only was Wendall Potts much smaller than his wife in stature and girth, but Janice was at least twice as long-winded and tedious as he was quiet and mild mannered. Joe gave each of them a cup of coffee then politely listened as Janice's nonstop blather continued for the next five minutes. As she jabbered on, Joe couldn't help but believe that Wendall Potts must have the patience of Job.

Finally, Judy came in with a tray of sandwiches and Joe thought that Janice would eat one and be silent. He was wrong! Somehow the woman managed to talk and eat without choking. Her long-suffering husband just passively sat there eating his sandwich and drinking the coffee while his wife's constant yakking seemed to numb the very air around her. Janice did, however, get Joe's attention when she said, "Vicky Sue Chase McClure was a good friend of mine. I never believed that she just took off and left her daughter. I still think that Jack had something to do with her disappearance, but I've never been able to figure out what happened."

Judy's guilty expression would have given her away if any of the others in that room had taken notice. From the kitchen Vanessa saw and wished she hadn't.

Janice didn't miss a beat as she kept blabbing and said, "Deidra could have at least made an appearance at her own father's funeral. We all know that she had it rough as a kid, but she should have been there."

Wendall Potts surprised everyone when he spoke loudly and said, "That poor girl was right to stay away! Jack McClure mistreated and neglected his daughter! And he sexually misused her! I saw it with my own eyes!"

Wendall was shaking as he recalled the day when he stumbled upon the horrific scene. He said, "That terrible man was forcing himself on his own daughter. Vince saw it too! He was looking for the puppy that you two gave him for his birthday when he was five years old. The boy had fallen into a low spot right next to where Jack attacked his daughter."

Wendall began to cry then said, "Later that day I told Jack what I had seen and that I was going to call the law. He told me that if I ever told anyone, he'd put me and my family where they put Vicky. When I asked Jack where Vicky was and who helped him, he grabbed me and threw me on the ground. Then he threatened to kill me. I stayed away from him after that." Wendall took out his handkerchief and wiped his eyes. Then he blew his nose and said, "I've lived with the guilt of knowing what Jack did to Deidra and the shame of my own cowardice for all these years." His face was ashen when he looked across the room at his dumbfounded wife and said, "Please forgive me for keeping this secret. I did it for you and the kids."

With their mouths gaped open, the others sat in stunned silence as they watched the emotionally broken man get up and walk out of the Chelsea home without saying another word. His usually chatty wife was frozen in her seat until she heard her husband start the car. Janice moved like a robot when she stood up from the chair and walked out to the waiting car.

Together the Chelsea's, including Vanessa, walked to the front door and watched the Potts' car drive away. After a moment, Joe looked at Judy and saw that all the color had drained from her face. He embraced the woman he loved and gave her a big, bear hug. Vanessa's strength abandoned her. She stumbled over to the chair that Janice had only recently vacated and sat down. Bewilderment flooded over her as she watched her parents gather the lunch dishes and take them to the kitchen.

While listening to the muffled sounds of the dishes bobbing up and down in the kitchen sink, Vanessa had time to absorb everything that Wendall Potts had said. The feebleness she was experiencing slowly began to lift only to be replaced by an understanding that caused her to feel a deep, aching guilt. Vanessa was finally forced to face what she had done. For too many years she had been unjustly directing her anger toward an innocent victim, Deidra. But the only two people who were responsible for what happened to Vicky McClure were Jack McClure and Vanessa's own mother. And she had helped them get away with it by keeping their terrible secret.

In the past Vanessa would have been seething with anger. But now she succumbed to the understanding of her own victimization. She realized that she had been living with debilitating confusion, fear and anger for far too many years. Feeling at last free of the need to constantly dwell on what she had witnessed long ago gave Vanessa the desire to make some changes in her life. Still, she wasn't sure what she should do next.

That night after Joe and Judy had crawled into their bed, he began to speak of the sudden disappearance of Vicky McClure many years earlier. Then he asked, "I wonder where Jack put Vicky and who helped him?" Judy couldn't answer. Her mind was totally occupied with trying to rationalize the treacherous deeds of her past.

The next morning was a Saturday. Vince and Deidra got up early and drove to the three-room shack where she'd been raised. They wanted to try and clean up the place. Also, they hoped to find something that could be salvaged. After Vince parked the brown pickup truck in front of the home, he noticed Deidra looking up at the television antenna. She was thinking about the lightning strike that had taken her father's life. Then she remembered that she had been the one to take the life of Margot

Burke. That recollection caused her to shiver. Vince didn't know why Deidra was shivering, but he did know that he wanted and needed to lean over and give her a hug. So, he did!

When they got out of the truck, Vince grabbed the cardboard boxes full of cleaning supplies and the two of them walked to the front door of the home. When Deidra opened it, they were instantly met with a stench that was so powerful they considered setting the place ablaze. But Deidra decided to put on her work gloves and press on with the hope of recovering something that might have belonged to her mother. Vince pursued his wife through the front door and began to gag. He had to turn around and leave. Deidra then asked him to back the pickup truck as close as he could to the front door so she could start throwing the garbage and trash that nearly filled the main room of that filthy hovel into the truck's bed. She stood by the door and took a deep breath before going to get some debris. After carrying out many armfuls of rubbish and dumping the stuff into the truck, Deidra had the largest room in the house that served as a combination kitchen and living room cleaned out except for a few pieces of old, wooden furniture and a dilapidated gas stove.

By then Vince had overcome his nausea and timidly entered the home again. He went into the small bedroom where Deidra had slept and was happy to report that although the room smelled a little funny, it didn't have an extremely offensive odor. But when he went into the larger bedroom, it reeked. Another wave of nausea overtook him so he ran outdoors and this time he upchucked.

Deidra followed her husband out and consoled him before going back into the house. She had to hold her breath when she went into the larger bedroom. She soon discovered that the old mattress her father had been sleeping on was the culprit creating the bad smell. Deidra awkwardly struggled with the stinky mattress until she got it outside. She knew that she couldn't lift it into the bed of the truck, so she dropped it on the ground. Deidra could only feel sympathy for her husband as she watched him lift that odious thing into the bed of his truck. After Vince accomplished that, it took a few minutes for him to recover from his third bout of nausea. Then he announced a great, big thank you to God for reminding him to bring a good pair of work gloves so that his hands didn't have to touch the grimy mattress. His prayer brought a smile to Deidra's face. Taking a cue from her husband, she gave thanks to God for providing her with such a brave husband. Her words caused Vince to giggle like a little boy.

That same morning Bryan Smith was part of a large crowd gathered in the town of Delite for the first little league baseball game in the newly refurbished community sports park where he had played as a boy. His brother-in-law, the Rev. Adam Applegate, said the plan that Bryan had drawn up and presented to the Young Adult's Church Group had been pivotal in making the field once again suitable for the children in the area. And it seemed as though the entire community had gotten behind it!

Bryan surveyed the new bleachers and could feel the excitement amongst the people seated there. As he looked around the ball diamond, he was really surprised by the large number of people who had chosen to bring their own lawn chairs. When he again looked up into the bleachers, he spotted Chelsea Swanson sitting next to his sister. He smiled when he remembered how sweetly Chelsea had explained to Haley that romantic feelings just didn't exist between him and Chelsea. Haley had been a little disappointed because her brother hadn't at long last found his true love, but was satisfied by his and Chelsea's decision to remain good friends.

With the vigorous call from the umpire to play ball, the game commenced. Bryan was as enthusiastic as the other fans during the game, but felt like something was missing. Then he thought about Margot Burke. That's when Bryan became very determined to not think about his past and direct his focus solely on the present ballgame and his future. When the contest was over, he personally congratulated the young players on both teams and their coaches for the good game they had played. He was actually feeling pretty good.

Then during his drive home, he realized that it was time for him to make an important change. Bryan stopped at a military recruiting station. He spoke briefly to a young Air Force sergeant who gave him some pamphlets to look over. That night Bryan decided that if he could pass the physical, he would leave his job at the electric company and enlist in the Air Force.

Monday morning rolled around fast. Vince and Deidra finished their morning chores then packed a sack lunch so they could return to her childhood home to do some cleaning. They were both glad when the smell of the place became quite a bit more tolerable after the kitchen sink was scoured and the woodwork and floors were thoroughly scrubbed. With the home almost completely disinfected, they both enjoyed sitting down and eating off the old, scratched up dinette set.

Vince asked Deidra if there was anything in the place that she wanted to keep and she pointed to an antique cabinet that had been made by her great-grandfather and his brother. He admired the workmanship of the cabinet then watched his wife dip a clean cloth into a bucket of water that had Murphy's oil soap in it. Deidra wrung it out and began to gently wipe the cabinet. Vince carefully tipped back the heavy piece of furniture so that his wife could clean under it, and that's when she spotted a hidden door. She dusted off the cobwebs and gently pulled on the knob of the door, but it wouldn't open. Vince laid the cabinet on its side so he could get a look at it. Then he found a keyhole and said, "It must be locked. I wonder where the key is?" That question triggered a memory that had lain dormant in Deidra's mind since she was only four years old.

"I know where it is!" she said. Then she jumped up and ran to her bedroom closet with Vince right on her heels. She tried to pry up the farthest floorboard on the right side of her closet. Deidra couldn't do it, but Vince tugged on it until the board came loose. He placed it aside then pulled out a small, puckered up leather pouch that was bound by a thin piece of twisted wire. Deidra said, "Mummy hid this in my closet before she went away. She told me that it was our secret and that I shouldn't tell anyone, not even my father." Vince unwrapped the pouch and discovered a small metal box. When he opened the box and found a key, Deidra said, "Mummy told me it was the key to her heart and said that someday I would use it to find love."

Vince took the key out and placed it in his wife's tiny hand, and then they went back to the cabinet. Deidra felt a little unsteady as she knelt down to put the key in the hidden door and give it a turn. Rewarded with the sound of a click, she carefully pulled the door of the hidden compartment open.

The two of them sat mesmerized for a long moment before Vince pulled out a faded cigar box and a small envelope. Deidra felt a spark of trepidation and winced when Vince tried to hand her the envelope.

He put the cigar box on the floor and placed the envelope on top of it before caressing his wife. Then he reached into the compartment of the cabinet and picked up the last item which was wrapped in canvas. He knew instantly what it was by the feel of it. He cautiously unwrapped the canvas and beheld an old pistol. The timeworn firearm had the name of Percifal S. Chase and the year 1861 engraved on its handle. Deidra softly said, "That man was my great-grandfather's brother. He and my great-grandfather made this cabinet before the Civil War. I remember my mother telling me that Percifal Chase carried this pistol during that war."

Vince gently placed the pistol back in the canvas and laid it on the floor. Then he reached for the cigar box. He looked to his wife who nodded for him to go ahead and open it. Inside the box was a bible. He carefully took the book out and opened the front cover. He heard his wife inhale deeply when she saw the name, Vicky Sue Chase McClure inscribed as the book's owner. Deidra's finger traced her mother's signature before she said, "This bible must be what Mummy meant when she told me that I would use the key to find love." Vince said, "The bible says that God is love in 1 John, Chapter 4, Verse... 8."

Vince's thumb wiped a tear as it began to fall down his wife's cheek and said, "Do you want to know what's in the envelope?" She shook her head yes so he gently opened it and said, "It's a photograph of you and your mother sitting in a sidecar of a motorcycle. There's also a letter to you from your mother." They studied the picture for a moment then they read the letter together.

To my beautiful daughter, Deidra Lynn Chase McClure:

I'm writing this letter to you on your fourth birthday. I want you to always know that I love you very, very much. You have brought so much happiness to me and you have completed me. Because of your presence in my life, I realize that I have been blessed by God. I pray that you will always stay as sweet and kind as you are now.

Love,
Mother

This letter in her mother's own handwriting caused Deidra to at last understand how much the woman who had given her life truly loved her. Suddenly, the intensity of her emotions made Deidra become lightheaded and she wavered. Vince picked his wife up and carried her out into the afternoon air. He took her to a shady corner of the yard and laid her down in a bed of fresh smelling grass so she could recover.

A few minutes later he helped her get back into the truck. Then he went to the house and retrieved the items that had been in the cabinet. As he closed the front door of the home he was mindful that Deidra wanted to keep the antique, but decided to have his father help him with the heavy piece of furniture at a later time. Then he thought that the only girl he had ever loved should never have to come back to this terrible place again.

Chapter 12

It was the first week of October 1969. James Burke felt he needed to get away by himself so he could do some fishing out in the Gulf of Mexico. When he told his parents what he intended to do, the looks on their faces told him they weren't exactly in agreement with his decision. James thanked them in advance for taking care of Teddy Whitefoot while he was to be gone then gave his mother a peck on the cheek before he climbed into his truck. His parents shielded their eyes with their hands because of the glare from the early afternoon sun and watched James drive out of their sight.

Lyle and Catherine went back into their home and were trying not to obsess over their son. Neither of them liked the idea of him being alone on the open water. They hovered over James' feline buddy and watched Teddy devour his food while each said a silent prayer for their son's safety.

Later that afternoon, James' energy level increased with each skip the rented pleasure craft took across the waves. After the land disappeared from his sight, he stopped and dropped the anchor. After massaging some of the anti-fungal cream into his hands that the doctor had given to him for his creepin' crud, James cast his fishing line over the edge of the boat from the stern. It was the perfect spot for catching fish, and that he did! He had caught several by the time he noticed that the sun was getting lower in the sky. He decided to go down to the galley and prepare a meal for himself. He saved a couple fish by putting them on ice, then cleaned and filleted one for his dinner. While the fish was poaching, James searched the cupboard for some salt because he had forgotten to bring any. He was delighted when he found a full container of it.

He also found a full bottle of tequila. Instantly, he recalled the horrible taste of the stuff that he'd sampled from a metal canteen in Southeast Asia. As James fingered the bottle, he wondered what tequila would taste like if it came out of a glass bottle instead of a metal canteen. Then he decided he really didn't want to know.

After a long day of doing chores within the mobile home park, Chelsea decided to be lazy and snack on peanut butter and crackers instead of going to the trouble of making herself a late afternoon meal. Sweetie seemed to be satisfied resting at Chelsea's feet until they heard a soft rap on the front door. Chelsea was surprised to see her father and Jane. They both looked upset. Chelsea understood why after they came in and her father said, "I just got off the phone with Andrea. I'm sorry to have to tell you that Michael has died in Southeast Asia."

Jane and Sam watched Chelsea collapse on the couch and begin to weep. In the blink of an eye, Sweetie jumped up and cuddled next to her. In that moment, all of the hurt Chelsea had endured during the time she was married to Michael seemed so insignificant. She was truly mourning for the loss of her first love. After a bit longer Chelsea said that she would be fine and was going to take Sweetie for a walk down by the water. Her father and Jane offered to go with them, but Chelsea said that it wasn't necessary.

They watched her put on the dog's leash, and then they walked with her as far as their home. Jane couldn't help but cry as Chelsea headed away from them and went out of their sight. Sam was in the grips of an almost crushing sadness and embraced his wife. He held her close and perhaps a little longer than he otherwise would have. But Jane understood and said, "Chelsea has a strong trust in God, Sam. She just needs some time." Then she cradled his hand in hers and said, "We better go in now, Honey."

When Chelsea reached the shoreline, she began to ponder the last hours that Michael and she had spent together while traveling to Pensacola. Even in her sadness she was able to realize that she had been greatly privileged by God to witness what a fine man he had become. With that understanding, she knelt down next to her dog and gave thanks to the Lord. When she stood again, she noticed that out to the west a storm was building up over the Gulf in the late afternoon sky.

Inexplicably, Chelsea suddenly knew that her intuitive abilities were in force when troublesome feelings began to plague her. She really wanted to dismiss them and told herself that what she was feeling was due to her grief because of Michael's death. But somehow she knew that something else was about to happen. And that caused Chelsea to feel very, very uneasy.

Out in the Gulf, James enjoyed the meal he'd prepared for himself and straightened up the galley. Then he laid down on one of the bunks and was soon dozing. He didn't realize anything was happening when he became slightly aroused by the tossing of the boat. But he became wide awake when a bright light with an accompanying loud clap of thunder shook his entire body.

James gingerly tried to stand up and was thrown to the floor by the severe motions of the vessel. He knew that he had a big problem, so he began to crawl toward the stairs.

When he reached them, he started to climb and was nearly to the top when a wave washed over the boat. A torrent of water doused him so he quickly grabbed onto the railing with both hands and pulled himself up to the deck. He managed to stand and was trying to reach the craft's controls when another wave came crashing over him. That's when James went overboard.

Chelsea and Sweetie ran all the way back to their mobile home. The dog watched its human friend get ready for bed then Sweetie nestled next to her. But they weren't able to stay in their bed. Sleep would not be with them this night. Even though they spent many hours either mindlessly watching television or listening to the radio, Chelsea was still nagged by the feeling that something was happening and whatever it was, was not good.

Finally, just before the sun came up Chelsea proved her faith and trust in God by giving her uneasy feelings to Him and praying. At last she felt unburdened and realized that this is what she should have done all along. Silently she gave thanks and asked for His loving forgiveness. When the sun came up she began to softly sing, 'What A Friend We Have In Jesus'. Even Sweetie seemed to be showing her appreciation for God's love by snuggling closer to Chelsea as she sang.

Out in the Gulf of Mexico, James was thanking God for the daylight. As he drifted in the early morning sunlight, he clung to the capsized boat and felt very grateful that it hadn't sunk during the previous nights' storm. Surveying his present surroundings and conditions, he was hopeful. The water was a lot calmer and the sky was clearing.

Physically he was exhausted and half nauseated because of all the seawater that he'd swallowed. James remembered that Chelsea Swanson had stuck her finger in the Atlantic Ocean so she could taste the saltiness of it. That brought a smile to his lips despite his current circumstances. Then he thought about the helicopter crash in Southeast Asia and wondered if he would soon be joining his good friend, Kevin Scoggins. As he yearned to be with his parents and Teddy Whitefoot he surprised himself by mustering a loud shot. "Don't give up! You're not dead yet James Burke!"

That same morning Joe and Vince Chelsea went over to Deidra's childhood home. After they had removed the antique cabinet and closed up the home, Joe decided to take a walk behind the house. Toward the back of the yard he saw an outhouse and a small wooden storage building. Both buildings appeared to be leaning. Curiosity spurred him through overgrown brush and rubble until he could see that the buildings were being propped up by boards.

Joe hoped that the storage building wouldn't fall over when he pulled on the door. He somehow managed to crack it open just far enough to look in. He was astonished when he spotted an old motorcycle and sidecar. It reminded him of the time he and Sam Swanson had borrowed a rig like this while they were stationed in Belgium during WWII.

As soon as Joe got back home, he phoned Sam Swanson. When Joe told Sam what he had found, Sam wondered aloud if the two of them would be able to make the motorcycle and its sidecar roadworthy.

Then Sam told Joe about Michael's death in Southeast Asia. Sam said that he was concerned for his daughter because Chelsea still had feelings for her former husband. Joe said,

"Maybe Chelsea shouldn't be alone right now." Then Joe suggested that it might be a good idea for the Swanson and Chelsea families to have a wiener roast and hayride out at the Chelsea ranch that evening. Sam said that he would check with his wife and daughter and promised to call Joe right back. Sam soon phoned and said that both of his ladies had accepted Joe's invitation with a big thank you from each of them. Then Sam said, "My ladies would like to know what they can bring and Chelsea asked if her dog can come along." Joe laughingly replied, "Bring your empty stomachs and the dog, too!"

Later that afternoon, Chelsea excitedly hurried home from her job at the bank. She was thrilled at the thought of seeing the Chelsea family and quickly changed into a T-shirt, jeans and sneakers. Since she had moved to Delite, she had only seen Joe and Judy Chelsea at her father's wedding and whenever they came into the bank. She remembered being a nine-year old and having so much fun when the entire Chelsea family had visited her family in Meadowview, N. Y. Chelsea was really looking forward to seeing Vince and Vanessa again. As for Sweetie, she somehow seemed to know that she was going to see some sights and smell some smells that she hadn't ever been privy to before.

By the time Sam, Jane, Chelsea and Sweetie arrived, Joe and Vince were standing next to a wood fire that already had a nice bed of hot coals. The friends were very happy to get reacquainted except for Vanessa. She stayed off to one side and purposely busied herself with whittling some sticks for the roasting of hot dogs and marshmallows.

Judy had the picnic table filled with trays of side dishes and beverages, but had to go back into the house to get the condiments, paper cups and plates. When she returned with the last tray, Judy couldn't find a spot on the table to put it. Chelsea saw that Judy needed help so she began rearranging the items on the table to make some space. Chelsea had her back to everyone and didn't see Vince's wife come walking over to him. When she finally turned around, the two young women locked eyes. Chelsea immediately rushed over to Deidra and said, "I know you! Do you remember me?" Chelsea looked at her father and Jane then said, "She helped me after my car accident!"

132

Deidra, Sam and Jane immediately knew what Chelsea was talking about, but the others didn't have a clue. Having never been told by Deidra that she had rescued a woman from a burning car, Vince turned to his wife and asked, "What's Chelsea talking about?" Deidra's voice was barely audible when she said, "It was no big deal."

Chelsea explained to Vince and his family that she had been involved in a serious automobile accident. Then she told them that she remembered feeling lightheaded but couldn't remember going off the road. The next thing she could remember was being on the ground some distance away from her burning car. Chelsea looked at Deidra and asked, "How did I get out of my car?" Deidra shyly replied, "I saw your car go off the roadway so I went over to see if you were okay. You were passed out behind the steering wheel. Then flames began to come out from underneath the car, so I grabbed onto you and dragged you away." It was obvious that Deidra was feeling a little self-conscious when she shrugged and said, "That's all."

Everyone there understood with certainty that Chelsea would have perished if it weren't for Deidra. Even Vanessa recognized that Deidra's presence at the exact time when Chelsea needed help couldn't possibly be a mere happenstance.

Jane had tears in her eyes when she went over to Deidra and said, "Thank God you were there. You saved our sweet Chelsea's life. Thank you." Then Jane gave Deidra a great, big hug. That's when Vanessa felt the tears welling in her own eyes. Feeling overwhelmed by emotions that didn't involve anger and hostility still seemed foreign to Vanessa. Embarrassed by what she perceived as weakness, Vanessa turned her head so that no one could see her cry.

For the rest of the evening, Vanessa watched intently as her brother's wife and Chelsea Swanson interacted. Without a doubt, Vanessa wanted to be able to have a relationship with another human being. But she just hadn't allowed herself to learn how to do that.

While everyone, especially Sweetie, enjoyed eating the roasted hot dogs, Chelsea noticed that Vanessa was paying close attention to her conversation with Deidra. Suddenly Chelsea felt an impalpable urging that she knew could only come from, His Holy Spirit, to specifically ask Vanessa if she would like to go with her to the next church service. Much to the surprise of everyone in her family, including Vanessa, she said yes.

Later Vince pulled the hay wagon nearby. Sweetie began to circle it and was looking for a spot that she could safely reach if she jumped up. The dog began to whimper when she realized that she couldn't leap that high, so Vanessa picked her up and put her on a hay bale. After Vanessa climbed on, she took Chelsea's hand and pulled her up. She then did the same for Deidra. Vince was incredulous when he saw his sister help his wife onto the hay wagon and wondered what had gotten into her.

During the hayride, Vince drove all over the Chelsea ranch. Sam was impressed by the large number of cattle that his old Army buddy and his family owned. Vanessa was holding onto Sweetie and was brought to laughter by the dog's antics. Every time Sweetie saw a cow she snorted and tried to wriggle out of Vanessa's arms. When Sam said, "Sweetie thinks she can get a bite of some steak while it's still on the hoof," Vanessa laughed even harder. And it felt good!

Deidra became very excited when Vince pulled the hay wagon next to the hog building and jumped off before he had the tractor stopped. With Vanessa distracted watching Deidra, Sweetie saw an opportunity to make a quick get away. The dog scrambled out of Vanessa's safe arms and ran into the building where she immediately challenged a large mother hog. After a rather loud and boisterous skirmish, Sweetie was either wise enough or cowardly enough to back off. She ran outside and hid behind a large tractor wheel. All the humans found humor in what the dog had done except for Chelsea. She checked to see that her dog was unharmed then attached the leash to her naughty doggy's collar so she couldn't get into any more trouble.

Deidra decided it would be best to bring one of the piglets out so the Swansons could hold it without its mother making a big fuss. Jane was the first to take the small, squealing critter in her arms. Cradling the piglet seemed natural to her because it reminded her of the year when her parents secretly raised one just like it in the small backyard of a house they rented during the depression. The landlord surely would not have appreciated it if he had known about the pig, but times were tough. Besides, her parents had hopes of selling the finest cuts of the pork to a local restaurant. They also wanted some of the meat for their own personal consumption.

Jane's father had tried to warn her not to become attached to the animal, but she had already named the pig, Rosie. Eventually, the inevitable day came for Rosie to be butchered. At the age of only six, Jane gritted her teeth and didn't cry even one tear as she watched a man load her pet in the back of his truck and drive away.

On the morning that her father brought home a small portion of the pork, Jane was determined to be very brave and eat the bacon that was placed next to the fried egg on her plate. She recalled how she had closed her eyes before taking the first bite. When she swallowed it, her father and mother told her how proud of her they were for being such a sensible girl. Jane handed the piglet to Sam and felt blessed by God for her childhood memories and for the happy memories that she and Sam would undoubtedly create together.

When the tour was over, Vince backed the hay wagon underneath the equipment shed then disconnected it from the tractor. After doing that, he saw his father and Sam coming toward him. Both were very animated as they talked. He saw Sam point to the motorcycle and sidecar on the other side of the shed and thought that they must be discussing their intention to restore them.

The three men were soon joined by the ladies. Vince noticed that Vanessa was looking at the old, gray 1947 Ford that had been parked in the shed since his grandfather, Nathan Chelsea, had passed away. He was more than a little puzzled when he heard his sister ask, "I wonder if Grampa's old car could be fixed up and made drivable?" Sam said, "I'm sure it would be fun to try!"

James saw that the sun was setting in the western sky and realized that he was likely facing another night floating in the Gulf. He couldn't decide if it was thirst or exhaustion that had him to the point of feeling utterly helpless. But determination for self-preservation bolstered James while he struggled with the constant movement of the water surrounding him. As he clung to the overturned boat, he thought about his life. James began to thank God for the innumerable and undeserved blessings that he'd been given. Undeniably, being raised by the finest sort of people, Lyle and Catherine Burke was at the top of his list. Then James fell asleep. Sleeping and waking was to happen again and again during this night. And each time he awoke, he was amazed to find that even while sleeping, he'd never let go of the boat.

After the Swanson family had gone, Judy and Vanessa were cleaning up the remaining food and trash from the picnic while Joe, Vince and Deidra went to check on the cattle. The mother and daughter worked silently as they took the leftovers into the kitchen. Judy had just put the last of them in the refrigerator when she turned to see that her daughter was giving her a look that could only be described as a stink-eye. Judy was about to ask her daughter why she was giving her such a mean look when Vanessa calmly said, "Mother, I saw what you did to Vicky McClure. I was looking in the window of the old shack down by the creek when you hit her over the head with a board."

Vanessa instantly saw the terror in her mother's eyes. Emotions that Vanessa couldn't identify began hurtling through her entire body and those passionate feelings seemed to be a conduit for an immobilizing, unhinged power. It came as a surprise to Vanessa when her limbs began to obey her mind's command to move as she slowly turned to walk out of the kitchen. She was thinking that all she needed to do was get to the safety of her bedroom while he was climbing up the stairs. Then she got into her room and immediately started to wrestle with why she was feeling so totally dissatisfied with being there. Her bedroom had always before caused her to feel safe. That insecurity threatened her even more when Vanessa realized that she really didn't have anywhere else to go. It was like she was attempting to wade through a river of rolling emotions that were drowning her.

On the following morning, the natural inclination for James to simply close his eyes because of the brilliant, blinding light reflecting off of the ever moving water relentlessly tried to lure him into giving up. But the tenacity of his spirit held fast onto what an unknown future in this world would set before him.

Meanwhile, Chelsea Swanson was in her usual morning rush mode. She quickly saw to Sweetie's needs then dressed in a T-shirt and jeans because she would be doing chores within the mobile home park. During their ride home from the picnic at the Chelsea Ranch on the previous evening, her father had said that they would probably be mowing, raking and gathering lawn debris. She really enjoyed the physical labor part of working in the park and thought that she had the best of two worlds. Chelsea thought of her job at the bank as being her clean girl job! She thought her job here in the park allowed her to get her hands dirty and she thought that was great too!

Chelsea was smiling as she gave Sweetie a pat on her head before walking out the front door. But while walking toward the mobile home park's office, Chelsea's smile disappeared. A vivid apprehension from an unknown source crept into her. She had the perception that the intuitive feeling she had experienced two nights ago was involved.

Then she remembered how the Lord had lightened her burden when she had asked Him in prayer to carry it for her! After Chelsea prayed and leaned on the Lord, her day went very well indeed!

The dismal night had seemed as though it would never end to Vanessa Chelsea. At last a ray of sunshine finally filtered through the wavy glass of her bedroom window. That light and her thoughts gave her the feeling of being lifted out of the depths of a great chasm. Complete understanding about the truth of her life was making her feel hopeful about her future and that caused Vanessa to be able to make a very important life decision. She couldn't keep from smiling as she quickly dressed then ran out to tell her horse and best friend, Manny, what she was going to do. Not realizing that she was racing through her morning chores on the ranch, Vanessa was feeling almost giddy, yet in control, by the time she met up with Vince and Deidra in the pig barn.

Over the sounds of the squealing pigs, a smiling Vanessa asked her brother if she could borrow his truck. Vince was surprised by his sister's request but told her that she could. Then Vanessa turned to her sister-in-law and asked, "Would you be willing to rent the home where you were raised to me?" Deidra looked shocked and asked, "Why do you want to live in that dump? It doesn't even have an indoor bathroom!" Seeing that Vanessa was being serious, Deidra agreed to let her sister-in-law live in the McClure home on the condition that there would not be a rent charge. When his smiling sister held out her hand, Vince gave her the keys to his truck. As Vince and Deidra watched Vanessa climb into the old brown truck and drive away, they were in a state of disbelief because his sister actually seemed to be happy!

Time contained no boundaries for James Burke because his senses had become dulled. Although he was conscious enough to know that fatigue engulfed every part of him, his imagination was causing him to believe that the limitless water seemed to be tearing at him with its salty tentacles. He lifted his head and looked in all directions, but couldn't see anything except for his watery prison. So, he closed his eyes and began to dream that a beautiful dark-haired girl and a bug-eyed Boston Terrier were happily floating with him.

An unwelcome, wet world surrounded him when he next opened his eyes. James could tell by the sun that it was early in the afternoon. He shut his eyes and wanted only to resume dreaming about Chelsea Swanson and her dog because he much preferred to imagine them than face his reality. When he began to dream again, it was not about the pleasant softness of a pretty girl. This time his dream was deafening as it thrust him back into the helicopter with Kevin in Southeast Asia. James could almost hear and feel the drumming of the metal blades as they whirled above him. He began to feel a stinging sensation on his face but couldn't understand why. When James opened his eyes, he realized that beads of water were pelting him. Then within the haze of his perception, James felt like he was being placed in a harness.

Before long he was in a helicopter where he came face to face with his past. James' mind momentarily toyed with the notion that he might be hallucinating, but the reality of what was actually happening became genuine when he looked into the eyes of the man who was bending over him. In a hoarse voice James managed to say, "Panther!" A look of recognition and surprise crossed the other man's face before he cried out, "Key Lime!"

Much later that afternoon, James was still being closely watched by the staff of the Almeda Hospital. As he lay in his hospital bed, he realized that he was a very lucky man. The fact that he was suffering from dehydration seemed to be the major concern of those seeing to his medical needs.

He closed his eyes for a brief moment. A soft rustling sound caused him to reopen them and the first thing that greeted his sight was the look of love and concern on the faces of his parents. It deeply bothered James that he had caused them worry and heartache. But Lyle and Catherine Burke were very gracious and told him not to give it another thought.

His mother pulled a chair next to his bed so she could sit and caress his hand. His dad made a funny comment about how wrinkled his skin looked because he'd spent so much time in the water. But they all knew that Lyle was only making an attempt at lightheartedness because he was trying to gloss over his own emotional reaction to nearly losing his son.

Before his parents ended their visit with James, his mother gave him a hug. Then it was his father's turn. Lyle actually had tears in his eyes and just couldn't let go of his son until a nurse came in to check James' vital signs.

James watched his parents leave as the nurse began to tenderly perform her duties. After she left, he laid there for about half an hour mulling over all the things that had taken place during the last three days. He turned his head toward the second story window of the hospital room and gazed out at the evening sky. James gave thanks to God for providing him with such loving parents and the opportunity to continue his life here with them. Then he thought that his simple prayer just wasn't enough in return for God's ample blessings. Before he drifted off to sleep his optimism for the future soared when he was brought to the understanding that he could achieve anything if it was within the Lord's will.

That same evening Vanessa Chelsea hadn't made it home in time to have dinner with her parents. Her worried father met her the moment she walked in the kitchen door. He asked her why she had borrowed her brother's truck and where she had disappeared to for the entire day. Then he wanted to know why she wanted to live in the old McClure place.

Vanessa walked to the refrigerator and spotted what was left of the roast beef her parents had for dinner. She took it out and began to slice a piece of the meat off. She could see that her mother was lurking in the kitchen doorway and was listening to every word that was being said. Vanessa made herself a sandwich and truthfully said, "I drove to town today and got a job working as a checkout in the Five and Dime store. I think it's about time for me to have a home of my own, so I'm going to move into the McClure place for the time being. I hope you and Mr. Swanson can get Grampa's '47 Ford running soon. In the meantime, will you please let me use your car so I can get back and forth to work?" Joe Chelsea answered, "Of course."

Vanessa's father still looked worried so she said, "Don't worry Daddy. I won't be too far away." Then she picked up her sandwich and started to walk out of the kitchen. She paused by her mother just long enough to glower at her, and then walked into the living room. Vanessa stopped at the foot of the stairs and in a tone of voice that only her mother could hear spat out the words, "I'm staying close by just in case someone is tempted to do something that someone shouldn't!" Judy recognized the unveiled threat and remained silent.

Joe was baffled and just couldn't understand what had gotten into his daughter. He heard her say something to her mother, but couldn't make out the words. When he asked his wife what Vanessa said to her, Judy panicked because of her quandary. Not knowing what else to do, she shrugged her shoulders and hoped that Joe wouldn't pursue the matter any further.

The next morning James had a visitor. He didn't even know the man's real name. James only knew him as, Panther. The man introduced himself and said his name was, Christian Moreaux. "Everyone calls me Chris." Chris paused then said, "I suppose you're wondering how we happened to find you." James nodded so Chris continued by telling him, "My brother and I work for Manos Transport, Inc. When we spotted the capsized boat, we decided to take a closer look." James remarked, "This makes the second time that you've rescued me. Thank you, again!"

Then James wanted to talk about their shared experiences in Southeast Asia. But Chris held up his hand signaling for James to stop and said, "We took an oath to never speak about..." James said, "When I was questioned about my experiences, I was told that we did not have anyone in North Vietnam." James thought for a moment then said, "I know what events took place, but there came a time when I began to question that they had actually happened." Chris said, "I'm sorry, James. But, I'm sure you understand." James did understand that they couldn't talk about what happened to them in Southeast Asia and said, "Yes, I do."

Right at that exact moment Chelsea Swanson was looking at a paper with the address of the lawnmower repair shop in Almeda that her father had given to her. She had offered to pick up a mower part for him and decided that since it was such a beautiful morning that she would take Sweetie along. When Chelsea found the shop she said, "I found it!" Sweetie jumped with excitement. But then Chelsea felt intimidated when she was confronted by the tiny parallel parking spot that she would have to squeeze her car into. It took her several tries before she managed to maneuver her car into place without bumping anything around it.

Chelsea was still feeling somewhat unnerved by what she considered the ordeal of having to parallel park and took no notice whatsoever of the surrounding area. She told Sweetie that she wouldn't be gone too long and to be a good doggy and stay. But when Chelsea opened the car door, Sweetie bounded right over her lap and jumped out. Then the naughty doggy ran across the street.

Chelsea rushed after the dog and almost caught her in front of a large door. When the door opened, Sweetie ran through it. The scene seemed rather comical to the two ladies who had inadvertently opened the door for the Boston Terrier, but Chelsea wasn't laughing!

She followed her dog into a long hall, and then lost sight of her. When Chelsea heard a man talking to another man about a dog he had seen running down the hall, she asked him which way it went. He said, "The dog got onto the elevator just before the door closed!"

Chelsea looked around and saw a sign that read, Fire Stairs. Once in the stairwell, she ran up taking them two at a time. When she reached the second floor, she heard a woman say, "The dog was hiding under the food cart! I don't know how it got there!"

By now Chelsea was completely frantic. Trying not to look conspicuous, Chelsea quickly walked down the hall and looked into every room she passed.

Christian Moreaux realized that the oath he had taken prevented him from even suggesting that he had ever been in North Vietnam with James, but then he decided to grasp James' hand and shake it while saying, "Good-bye Key Lime."

When he walked to the room's entrance he stopped and turned around to face James. Then with his eyes full of expression and an ornery grin on his lips he softly said, "Quack, quack! Quack, quack, quack!"

In the midst of James' quacking response, a small Boston Terrier ran between Chris Moreaux's legs. Then the dog bolted up onto the bed that was occupied by a very startled James Burke!

Soon after, the surprised fellow standing in the doorway of the hospital room had to quickly step aside or be bowled over by a beautiful, dark-haired young woman! The woman dashed by Chris Moreaux and over to the foot of the hospital bed where she suddenly stopped in her tracks and exclaimed, "James!" The stunned man replied, "Chelsea!"

142

THE END

Epilogue

James Burke and Chelsea Jo Swanson were married on December 18th in 1969. On April 23rd of 1971, God blessed them with a set of twins. They named their daughter, Sharon Marie and their son Steven James. Both sets of grandparents and their Aunt Marie never missed a chance to spend time with the children!

A Personal note from the Author

The previous story was imaginary and many of the circumstances depicted were far beyond tolerable. There were times when the characters in this book struggled through their daily lives and with making important life decisions. There were also times when the determinations they made weren't good for them or for the other characters. During the reality of our own lives, our journey may take us through a tug-of-war with our own needs and desires and those of other people, worldly influences and what God would have us think, say and do. It's so easy to become discouraged, especially when we're hurting. But our situation is not hopeless! By choosing to remember that our Lord beckons us with His gracious love through the presence of His Holy Spirit, and by humbly trusting Him and using His road map, the Bible, as a guide, it's possible for us, even with our imperfections, to be comforted by our Lord while endeavoring to live a life that is pleasing to Him. May God bless you while you are preparing to spend your eternity with Him!

www.ingramcontent.com/pod-product-compliance
Lightning Source LLC
Chambersburg PA
CBHW051841170626
46807CB00003B/1288